Pandora

An American in Prague

A Novel

Zoë Myonas

WEST HILLS PUBLISHING

Thus your soul, set afire

By the lightning of desire

Flies, swift and fearless

Into the vast enchanted sky.

Then it spills, dying

In a flood of quiet sadness

To the bottom of my heart.

> *~ Charles Baudelaire*

one

Pandora wasn't used to being ignored. And it wasn't just that she was so beautiful, or that she was a stylish green-eyed American in a nation only now growing accustomed to American expatriates living and working among them. It was because her husband was watching a video while his sweet little wife was sucking his cock.

Ty loved it when she did this and was clearly enjoying it now, at least on some level as evidenced by his soft moans in sync with her expert fellation. She knew this was in no small part because of how good she was at it. In fact, she suspected it was one of the reasons he'd married her. The first night they made love, Ty had asked her if it was OK if he came in her. She'd replied it probably wasn't a good idea, since she hadn't been dating anyone and gone off the pill but she said he could finish in her mouth. After he made her come three times (who's counting?) she'd rested her arm over his belly and taken his by now impossibly hard cock in her mouth. The volume of his ejaculate had caused her evident surprise, he assumed unpleasant, and he offered to get her some water. Her blithe response was that it wasn't necessary, "I like the way it tastes." The poor guy was toast.

So how to explain their current circumstance? As she licked the bulging veins on his huge throbbing erection, she looked up into his eyes, staring raptly at the screen. Maintaining rhythmic oral manipulation, she turned her head to the wide blue screen to see what was holding his attention. It was an erotic video of a man with a penis as big as a baby's arm fucking a young woman with extravagantly large breasts doggy-style, while the young woman's head was buried between the legs of a second young woman, with ginormous surgically endowed breasts, lying on her back (are we clear on the logistics here?). The threesome seemed to Pandora to be going about their respective tasks with all the enthusiasm of supermarket checkers but mostly she was struck by the poor taste and shabbiness of the bedroom furnishings.

Things did seem to be picking up, however, and as the rutting trio began wailing and moaning in rude harmony Ty started to show signs that he was pulling into the station. Eyes riveted on the screen, he pushed his fingers into her hair, holding her head tightly as he forced her mouth down onto his cock, and she took it expertly into her throat, which brought tears to her eyes, delighting her as she felt the entirety of its throbbing in time with his shaking body and his screams. She looked up, wiped her lips and smiled, asking unnecessarily if it had been OK. Combing her hair with his fingers, he said, "You put me on the moon."

Still the porn stars droned on behind her. She looked back at them, now joined by another erect player, a hairy man with a prolapsed stomach. "So can we shut that off now?" she inquired. Getting no response, she looked at her husband, who was fast asleep, a happy little smile playing on his lips. Pandora remembered her mother quoting Fran Lebowitz during the post-grad phase of their birds & bees training, "Friends come and go; men come and go to sleep." She found the remote and switched off the video orgy.

Pandora lay back beside her husband, pulling up the sheet and blanket. She regarded his beatific smile and listened to his rhythmic breathing, thinking about their first date, when he told her Ty wasn't short for Tyrone but Tibor, that it had been his grandfather's name, and that his twin brother Tom wasn't Thomas but Tomáš, and she marveled at how much these tiny bits of information had meant for their future. She thought about how much she had loved saying the words "Mrs. Krizova," and the first time she'd shown her wedding ring to a bore who had started into a familiar pickup routine while staring not-so-subtly at her breasts. She thought about how excited Ty had been to return to Czechoslovakia after the Velvet

Revolution, and the opportunities he saw that would make it more than worthwhile to leave their beautiful home in Santa Barbara. But mostly she thought about how he'd seemed to be more interested in three sleazy strangers' sexual calisthenics on a nasty-looking orange bedspread than his darling wife sucking his cock.

"Ty?"

Getting no response, she stroked his face.

"Ty?"

Ty murmured, "Yes, Panda" as he rolled over and buried his face in the pillow.

"Ty, you asleep?"

His reply mixed with a yawn, "Not anymore. Something on your mind?"

"I was thinking about that video we watched tonight. The thought of having sex with two women at the same time really turns you on, doesn't it?"

Ty rolled onto his back, resigned to the conversation. "I guess."

"You guess? Based on the load you shot into my mouth, I'd say that's an understatement."

"You always say you like it."

"I love it but that's not exactly the point, is it?"

Ty checked the emergency exits. "I have a feeling there isn't any safe answer to that question."

"Just tell me the truth. That's all I ever asked."

"OK, you're right, it's a turn-on."

She lay back against the pillow. "Is this something new?"

"Not really."

"Have you ever actually, you know, done it?"

"Another one of those questions."

She put her hand on his. "Just tell me. I love you, nothing you could say could change that, at least about something as stupid as this."

"OK, yeah. A few times."

Pandora sat up, incredulous. "A few times? How many is a 'few'?"

"I don't know, I'd have to think about it."

"You don't even know how many times?"

"There, that's exactly why I didn't want to tell you."

"I'm sorry, you're right, I shouldn't judge. Why haven't you ever said anything before if this is so important to you?"

He shook his head. "Because it's not that important to me, and I guess I was worried how you'd react. With good reason evidently, you're clearly upset."

Pandora pouted. "Maybe a little. It's like I'm not enough for you."

"Man, is that ever not true." He put his arm around her and pulled her to his chest. "Anyway, when I think about it, it's always something we're sharing."

"Oh, that makes it tons better. You imagine me making love to another woman with you?"

"Sometimes. Sometimes we're making love to you. Like when I enter you from behind and touch your pussy with my fingers? I sometimes think another woman is licking your clit while I'm fucking you."

"Wow."

"You've never thought about it? Like when you're in your shop and watching all those women try on lingerie?"

"Mostly I wonder if they're going to buy something or leave a wad of merchandise in the dressing room for me to hang up."

§

Pandora came out of her favorite coffee bar with coffee and a pastry bag and walked toward her shop on Pařížská Street, enjoying the bright spring morning. She wished she could have had breakfast with Ty, but he had international calls to make and had left their apartment before six. The only time they ate breakfast together lately was Sunday, and even then he frequently had an early tennis match. She especially regretted not seeing him this morning because of their awkward late-night conversation. She hadn't decided if it was something they needed to talk about more, or if it would be better left alone. After all, it wasn't like he was acting on these fantasies and in a way she was reaping a sort of dividend from them. Ty was unfailingly interested in sex.

The city was waking up, in every sense of the word. When they had first arrived she garnered stares every time she left the apartment, now no one looked twice at a leggy woman in heels. Well, almost no one. She turned onto Pařížská and crossed the street to her little shop with its art nouveau scripted sign spelling out "*Pandora's Box*" in English. No matter how many times she turned the corner and saw it, she always felt thrilled, like she was dreaming.

Two middle-aged women in designer yoga suits were looking in her window as Pandora approached the store. Definitely tourists. One of them squinted at her as she juggled her coffee and pastry to get out her keys. "Oh good, she's opening." Pandora opened the door and stepped back to admit them, and they made for the racks like piranha fish as she turned the "*Zavřeno*" sign to "*Otevřeno*" in the door.

Pandora put her coffee and pastry by the register, opened an envelope and filled the cash drawers. Normally she would have said something to the women, like "That rack is on sale," or "If you see something you like that's not your size I can try to order it for you," but one heard the most interesting things from people when they assume you don't speak their language, and these two didn't disappoint.

"Can you believe she didn't know?" said the woman who had spoken outside the store. "Suddenly he's 'working late' five nights a week, a guy whose idea of work is drinking with clients on the golf course."

"If Bob got a secretary who looked like that I'd have her out of there so fast she wouldn't know what hit her."

"He had sex with her in their bed. Can you believe that?" said the first.

"I believe it," clucked the second. "It's lucky she didn't leave them a present."

"What do you mean? Oh, God, you mean...don't be gross."

Pandora smiled to herself as she opened her coffee and removed the pastry from its paper wrap. The first woman selected a bra from the rack and showed it to her friend. "This is nice."

"It's OK," replied her friend, regretting that she hadn't seen it first.

The first woman held it up in Pandora's face, speaking slowly and loudly so as to be understood by this exotic foreigner, "DO YOU HAVE THIS IN A THIRTY-FOUR D CUP?"

Pandora smiled sweetly, resisting the urge to reply in kind, "I believe I have one left. It's in the back, I'll just check for you," she said in her California English.

"Oh, you speak American," said the surprised woman, "and so well. You sound like you could be American."

"I am," said Pandora from the stock room, "Santa Barbara. Well, Los Angeles, actually but my husband and I had a home in Santa Barbara before we came to Prague."

"It's so pretty here," said the woman. "We're from Chicago. It's always fucking freezing or fucking hot."

Pandora brought out two bras, giving her one. "I actually have it in black in a thirty-four D also."

"Oh, I'd like to try it too," her friend said, snatching the second bra from her fingers before the woman could speak.

"The dressing room is through that curtain," said Pandora. As she took a sip of coffee the phone rang. "Pandora's Box," she said brightly. The line was quiet. "Hello?" she said. Then the breathing began, heavy and coarse. "Oh, my goodness," said Pandora, "it's The Creepy Breather." She turned her back to the dressing room and lowered her voice. "Maybe you should call the silicone sisters from the porn video; they'd probably love all that hot and sweaty panting. Anyway, I have customers."

"I'm sorry, I'm sorry, I'm sorry," Ty said. "What can I do to make it up to you?"

"I'll think of something." She lowered her voice even more, "but I promise if you heard these women, it would definitely shatter your fantasy about me getting it on with my customers."

The doorbell dinged and a stunning woman with long straight dark hair, sprayed-on Spandex workout togs hugging her curves, entered the shop.

"Gotta go, another victim has entered my web, and this one is more in line with your fantasy."

"Our fantasy," said Ty.

"Dream on, Porn Boy."

"Sic 'em, Panda. Love you."

"Love you more," she said. Pandora hung up the phone and smiled at the young woman as she browsed a rack of negligees. The girl didn't look like a tourist, so she spoke to her in Czech. "You look for something special?"

The woman flashed huge eyes and smiled, answering in heavily French-accented English. "I am always looking for something special."

"Is my Czech really that bad?" Pandora laughed.

"Maybe like my English." The girl selected a black lace camisole. "You have such pretty things. I am so happy to find you."

"They're mostly French."

"I can see this."

"Like you?" said Pandora.

"Yes, I am from Paris but I haven't been home in...ooph, two years? I miss it but Prague is nice, very friendly to me."

"I can imagine," Pandora smiled, "I'm surprised I haven't seen you before."

"Oh, I haven't been in Prague in a while. I've been Moscow two, almost three years?" She made a serious face and lowered her voice. " *Я покупать ты водка?*"

"Is that Russian?" asked Pandora.

"Very," said the girl in English. "It means can I buy you drink? It's how men say hello to you there."

"It's how they say hello everywhere," said Pandora.

The two women came out of the dressing room, dumping a wad of tried-on undergarments in a chair on their way to the register. The first woman handed Pandora the bra she found for her in the stockroom. "Is this on sale?"

"Sorry, I just got it in," said Pandora.

The woman turned to her friend, "What do you think?"

"It looked great on you. But if it's not on sale—"

The first woman considered the bra, clearly a difficult decision, given her deep-set aversion to full price.

"Screw it, let's go. I need a Bloody Mary." She gave Pandora a weird smile as she tossed the bra on the counter. "Thanks anyway, I'll think about it."

As the door dinged behind the departing tough customers, the dark-haired girl smiled at Pandora, "You are very, how you say, *politique*?"

"It's the first lesson of retail," said Pandora.

"I'm Cerise," the girl said, offering her hand.

"I'm Pandora."

"And your shop is the Pandora's Box! I love this. How are you coming to have such a charming shop in Prague?"

"My husband is Czech but lived in America since he was a boy. His family had quite a bit of property before the, you know, the communists and all, and after the revolution he had some very good opportunities here. Part of the deal when he brought us here was I could have a shop, and I love lingerie, so..."

"The Pandora's Box."

"What do you do?" Pandora asked as Cerise added another camisole to the stack on her arm.

"You might say I am the entertainer." Cerise indicated the curtain, "Is that your trying-on room?"

"Just through there. Let me make sure my Americans didn't leave half the store back there."

Pandora pulled the curtain aside and saw more wadded-up lingerie on the chair spilling onto the floor.

"Sorry," said Pandora, "just let me get these."

"This must drive you crazy," said Cerise.

"It's not the part I fantasized about when I dreamt of having a shop," said Pandora, smiling as she thought about all the fantasy talk she and Ty had been having.

She carried the items out and Cerise entered the tiny space and hung her selections on the hook, stripping off her top without closing the curtain. She wasn't wearing a bra, and Pandora could definitely see why some people would find her entertaining. She thought about telling her she could close the curtain but the moment felt awkward and, anyway, it seemed a little late for that. Panda spoke as she sorted and rehung the earlier customers' items.

"What kind of entertainment do you do?" asked Pandora.

"Very personal."

"Sorry, I'm not usually so nosey."

Cerise laughed, "Oh no, I meant the entertainment I do is of the personal nature."

"That sounds interesting."

"Oh, very." Cerise was on to a lacy push-up bra. "Can you help me here?"

"Of course," said Pandora, squeezing in behind her as Cerise studied herself in the mirror.

"Is there a matching thong for this bra?"

"No, I think it's, like, a boy short. Do you know what I mean?"

"Oh, yes, I love these," said Cerise. "Is this fitting me correctly? The straps feel tight."

"They adjust easily."

"Could you help me?"

"Of course," said Pandora, as she adjusted the straps. "Is that better?"

"Yes, much," said Cerise, as she turned to face Pandora, very closely in the small space. "Do you like this on me?"

This caught Pandora off guard. "Yes. You're beautiful...I mean in that...it's beautiful on you. I can find the panties for it."

Cerise took another bra from its hanger. "No, please, first help me with this one? I couldn't get it open, I think my nails are too long?"

"OK," said Pandora, the intimacy of the situation beginning to get to her. She unhooked the bra and helped Cerise put it on. Cerise bent over and cupped her breasts to maximize the lift, then turned again to face Pandora. "So," she said, "which one do you like best?"

Lightheaded, Pandora hesitated. "They're both lovely on you. This one is a little more expensive."

"No matter," said Cerise, "it is the business expense. I'll take them both. Does this one also have matching panty?"

"What? Oh, yes," said Pandora, snapping out of her reverie, "and I think it's a thong."

"Wonderful," said Cerise. She looked at Pandora, who had stopped with her hand on the first rack. "Are you OK?"

"Sure," said Pandora, "I was just...it's nothing." She went to the shelf to look for the matching thong to Cerise's new bra.

"So, I'm really curious. What exactly is this 'very personal' entertainment? I mean, if you don't mind telling me."

"Not at all, I'm definitely not the shy person," said Cerise, "I dance."

"You mean you're a, like—" Pandora hesitated, afraid to offend her.

"*Stripteaseuse*? How you say, streepaire?"

"God, I'd never have dreamt that, you're so elegant, so beautiful."

"Thank you but isn't that the point? This is what they like. I first was in Moscow to dance; this was my dream since I was the very little girl. But one day the little girl got these big teats, and bye-bye ballet Russe. The master called me *'la petite vache*.' Little cow! *Le putain pédé!"* Cerise spit out the last words as she chose another bra.

"Well, sometimes a door closes, another one opens, no? I discovered there is the other kinds of dancing where these teats are very good."

Pandora found the thong and collected Cerise's other items. "I always thought of those clubs as being...sleazy?" she said as she took Cerise's selections to the counter.

Cerise laughed. "Oh, I don't dance in the club like this, with the pole and the bad smells and the money stuffed in my panties. Only private party, and only the best. Very expensive."

Pandora folded Cerise's new lingerie. "What do you have to do?"

Cerise pulled her top back on as she left the dressing room and walked to the counter. "Just the slow sexy dance." She mimed disrobing. "And the lap dance, if they are very good boys."

"Do you ever, you know—"

"Have the sex? Sometimes later I let them call but only if they're, ooh, so handsome, you know?"

"So they're not all old and creepy?"

"I wish they were. It would be easier for me to say no. I am like the child in the candy store. Sometime I think I like this too much. Does this sound terrible?"

She took her wallet from her purse and brought out a wad of bills.

"No," said Pandora, accepting the money. "You enjoy what you do, and you make living from it. What could be better?" She opened the register and made change as Cerise picked up a framed photograph.

"Your husband?"

"Yes, that's Ty," said Pandora.

"*Très beau*, you're a lucky girl," said Cerise. "Does he have a brother?"

"A twin brother but he lives in New York, and he's very married."

"*Pas mal*," pouted Cerise, "this is my luck."

§

Pandora often looked forward to bedtime with Ty but after Cerise departed with her new lingerie, promising to stop in regularly to see what lovely new items Pandora had received, she was <u>really</u> looking forward to it, and found herself wistfully checking her watch more than once. Of course it didn't occur to her that helping Cerise in the tiny dressing room had anything to do with that. Ty wanted to make love almost every night, sometimes twice, which was her favorite, waking from a deep sleep with him already inside her. But he was playing handball that night, and this sometimes left him so spent he was asleep as soon as his head hit the pillow. No worry. She had ways.

Ty was relieved not to have to discuss the previous night's disagreement over the light supper she saved for him and, indeed, was out nearly from the moment he crawled into bed. The hot shower hadn't helped. Pandora kissed him on his slightly open lips. "Ty?" she murmured. Getting no response she ventured south, kissing his cock as she scratched his balls with her flawless red nails.

Now it was Ty who murmured her name, "Pandora?" But if he hoped for sleep he was out gunned. She took the little fire helmet crowning his thickening member in her mouth, and it swelled into a considerably larger little fire helmet as he ran his fingers through her hair. She kissed his belly.

"God, Pandora," he said, rock hard now, "I love you." She worked her way back up to his chest, then kissed him hard on the mouth as she slid her pussy on his throbbing member, then pushed the tip between her other lips. He tried to thrust into her but she made him wait, wetting it little by little until the shaft was deep inside.

Now she righted herself, her full weight pushing him deeper inside her, and rolling her hips to grind her clit against his pubic bone. She arched her back, eyes closed, moving on him faster and he ran his hands from her hips to her breasts. And suddenly Cerise was behind her, kissing her neck as she reached around to her breasts. Pandora turned her head and their lips met, Cerise's tongue probing, promising other delights. And in that moment, Pandora climaxed so violently she nearly passed out, then collapsed on Ty's chest.

"Goodness," said Ty, "that sounded intense."

"Goodness had nothing to do with it," said Pandora, still out of breath.

"What?" he said.

She kissed him on the mouth. "That was really good."

"What came over you?" he asked.

She rested her head on his chest, eyes sparkling. "I don't know."

two

Cerise dropped her thick white cotton robe to the floor and pushed a perfectly pedicured foot through the mass of bubbles overflowing the huge tub, then settled into the steaming bath with a sigh. She rested her head and looked out the floor-to-ceiling French doors to the balcony overlooking the Vltava river. Cerise loved her life, and she was a lucky girl. When she arrived in Prague she'd more than enough saved from her Russian odyssey to get this wonderfully extravagant apartment, confident it wouldn't take her long to find a short roster of gentlemen to support her in the manner to which she was accustomed. And Prague had not disappointed.

She took a sip of Champagne from the flute on the table beside the tub and picked up the business card, turning it over in her fingers thoughtfully. Then she picked up her cordless phone and dialed the number.

Pandora was ringing up a sale for a customer when the phone rang. "Pandora's Box," she said, the phone wedged between her head and shoulder so she could continue writing up the receipt.

Cerise smiled when she heard the response on the phone's speaker.

"Allo' Pandora, this is Cerise. Are you remembering me?"

She put the phone down on the table and took another sip of Champagne.

"Of course," said Pandora. "Did those things work out?"

"They are the biggest hit," said Cerise. "I'm going to be your most wonderful customer."

Pandora's current customer handed over her charge card and she ran it through the press as she spoke. "I just got a box from Paris. Do you know the designer Assia Moireaud?"

"*Absolutement*," said Cerise. "You will find me the biggest expert in these matters. I will try to come in soon but I'm calling about the different matter. Some friends are having a party on the river Saturday." She lifted a slender foot above the bubbles and scrutinized her brightly lacquered toes. "You must come...I mean, you and your gorgeous husband, of course. I have ask them to send you an invitation."

"I'd love to come but Ty is playing tennis Sunday morning," said Pandora. "And it's business, the guy's a minister he's been working with."

"Perhaps you will convince him it will be worth staying up a bit late. I'm sure you have him, how do you say, wrapped over your finger?"

Pandora laughed as she returned her customer's credit card and gave her the voucher to sign. "He doesn't think so, and it's better that way. But I'll try, I promise."

"And wear your most sexy dress. I'm only allowed to invite my most beautiful friends. Ciao, Pandora," she said.

"Ciao, Cerise," replied Pandora. She returned the phone to its cradle, then put the charge voucher in the register and gave the customer her purchase. "He's going to love it," she said. As the customer left the store Pandora gave the phone a worried look. Of course she had <u>nothing</u> to wear.

That night Ty entered their apartment to find Pandora, dressed in a tank top and jeans, hard at work in her tiny converted-closet office, so focused she didn't hear him enter. He quietly stalked her, then kissed her neck, cupping her breasts.

"Oh, God," she said, "you're not helping."

"The gods help those who help themselves," he said. He slipped his hands under her top, where they were instantly greeted by Pandora's always enthusiastic nipples. "And don't try to tell me you don't like it, 'cause the girls say otherwise."

"I have to write these orders tonight or I won't have any stock for summer," said Pandora.

Ty scowled at her breasts. "Liars."

She grabbed his head and kissed him. "They're telling the truth but unfortunately they can't write purchase orders."

He sighed, straightened up and stretched. "You'll know where to find me if they manage to change your mind."

"I won't be much longer," she said. "By the way," she added as he walked toward their bedroom, "one of my customers invited us to a party Saturday night. I told her you have a tennis match early Sunday so we probably couldn't..."

"Fine," Ty interrupted.

Pandora was surprised. "You sure? What about your big deal and the minister?"

"Panda," he said, "one of the advantages of not being a big drinker is I can almost always pull myself out of bed. I'm just glad you have a friend here, and you're thinking about something besides work. Now hurry up and finish that, and come to bed."

§

The week passed in a whirl. Pandora managed to find the perfect little black dress and, of course, lingerie (important because the dress was more than a little revealing) was no problem. Saturday night found them waiting dockside, Pandora in her new dress and four-inch heels, Ty in black tie with a plain black Armani suit. He was OK with the wing-collar shirt and bow tie but didn't like tuxedos--he hated the idea someone might ask him to fetch them a drink or request "Tie A Yellow Ribbon" during the band's break. Pandora saw him check his watch for the tenth time.

"Stop looking at your watch, we're supposed to be having fun."

"I am having fun."

"Really."

"Yeah, I like looking down the front of that dress."

"Oh, God, should I go back and change?" Pandora said, suddenly worried.

"Stop it, you look great," Ty said.

"Then you can stop looking at your watch."

"OK," he said, "but where's the fucking boat? The invitation—"

"Was in Czech," she interrupted. "In which case—"

"All times are approximate," he said, finishing their mutually constructed sentence. Then they heard the whistle and saw the little steamboat, gaily decorated with colored lights, its deck packed with partiers.

The boat reversed its engine as it approached, then bumped to a stop. The gangway clattered down onto the dock and Pandora and Ty walked into Cerise's crowded world.

As Ty led Pandora up the gangway, a tall, ripped, very handsome, slightly drunk gentleman in a tuxedo pushed his way passed them down the gangplank, nearly tipping Pandora into the river.

"Hey, what the fuck?" Ty called after him but the guy was oblivious and quickly gone.

As they stepped onto the boat Cerise hurried over to them, her face wet with tears. She extended her hand to Ty.

"I'm Cerise, I'm so happy you could come."

Pandora hugged her. "Are you OK?"

"I'll be OK," she answered.

"Was that guy with you?" asked Ty.

"He was, past tense," she said.

"What's his problem?" Ty asked.

"It's obvious," said Cerise, "he's *un* asshole."

The steward lifted the gangway and signaled the captain, who blasted the whistle as they got underway. "Come on, we'll get you freshened up," Pandora said, grabbing Cerise's arm. "Get us drinks?" she said to Ty.

Pandora said, "Where's the Ladies'?" as she steered Cerise through the crowd. Cerise pointed the way. "Your boyfriend?" asked Pandora.

"Not anymore," shrugged Cerise.

"Too bad, he's gorgeous."

"Well, I definitely wasn't seeing him for his personality. You obviously like the pretty boys too."

"Ty's not just nice on the outside," said Pandora.

"I never seem to get the whole package," said Cerise as they reached the powder room. "Anyway, he's rich, so two out of three is not so bad, no?"

Pandora tried the door. It was locked. Then she noticed one of Cerise's cheeks was glowing redder than the other. "He hit you!"

"It's nothing. Anyway I got him better. I kicked him in his balls."

"Wow, don't mess with Cerise."

"You better believe it, baby."

The door opened and a redheaded woman with a towering bouffant hairdo teetered out on stiletto pumps. The girls entered. "Why did he slap you?" Pandora asked, locking the door behind them.

"I told you, because I kick his balls."

"You mean you did it first?" asked the incredulous Pandora. "What did he do?"

"He called me whore. I'm not a whore," Cerise said, savagely. "I do what I want, with who I want. If they want to help me out, it's their business. If they don't it's mine if I stay or go."

She studied her face in the mirror. "Do you think will be a, how you say, *contusion*?"

"Bruise," said Pandora. She held her friend's chin in her hand and turned her face to the light. "No, I think it will be OK." She opened her purse and brought out makeup. "We'll just fix your mascara and put a little powder on. Here, lean against the sink."

"You speak French?" asked Cerise, complying, "or do you just know the word for bruise for some reason?"

Pandora answered in French, and they continued in that language. "It was my major in school. Lucky, because I do all my buying in Paris. You French are delightful but sometimes perhaps a little less so with Americans who don't speak French."

"No one is perfect. Why didn't you tell me this?"

"Your English is fine."

"Ooph, my English is terrible," said Cerise, "I sound like a cretin."

"Not at all," said Pandora, as she gently re-applied Cerise's mascara.

"Ah, don't you love this, when someone does your face?" said Cerise dreamily. "When I have photo shoots, having my makeup done is my favorite part. I could feel your touch all night."

Pandora wasn't sure how she felt about that, especially in the light of her vividly imagining Cerise being with them that night as she had made love with Ty. She snapped the mascara brush back into its tube and opened her compact. "A little powder, and you'll be good as new," she said as she gently daubed it on. "There," said Pandora, as she clicked the compact shut and dropped it into her purse.

"*Rouge à lèvres?*" said Cerise as she took her lipstick from her bag.

Pandora pulled the black-lacquered cap from the tube and gently pressed the crimson shaft to Cerise's pouting Botticelli lips, aware of how close they were to her own, and that now familiar feeling warming her. "There," she said, wondering if Cerise felt it too as she replaced the cap and returned it. "Let's find my date, and someone pretty for you."

"I think my choices may be limited by my karate show earlier. Anyone who didn't see it has heard about it by now."

"Oh dear," laughed Pandora. "Men *are* sensitive about kicking in that area, aren't they?"

"The big babies."

They reentered the crowd, pushing their way to the bar, where they found Ty holding court with a fifty-something gentleman in an older, slightly shabby tuxedo.

"This is Georg," said Ty, in English. "We're hoping to do our project with his firm." He nodded to Georg, "My wife, Pandora, and her friend Cerise."

"Very charmed," replied Georg, with a thick Czech accent, taking Pandora's hand. Then he smiled at Cerise. "Twice as charmed."

The woman behind him, her frumpy frock definitely pre-revolution, intruded, pushing her way in front of him, "And I am Georg's wife."

"*Enchenté*," said Cerise. "You are a very lucky woman." She turned to Ty and spoke loudly enough to be sure Mrs. Georg heard, "Who does a girl need to fuck in this place to get a drink?"

"Well, I'm sure that won't be necessary," laughed Ty. He spoke as he handed Pandora a glass of Chardonnay, "What would you like?"

"A dirty martini, please," she replied.

"Me too," said Pandora.

Ty signaled the bartender, who leaned over for their drink order, which included another beer for himself. Then he raised an eyebrow to his wife regarding Cerise's question. Pandora shrugged, "That's Cerise."

"I like her," he said, "she's funny."

The bartender put the beer and the martinis on the bar. Ty tipped him and gave the girls their drinks.

"Who are our hosts?" he inquired of Cerise.

"I don't know," she answered, "my boyfriend got us invited."

"The gentleman we encountered when we were boarding?"

"He's certainly no gentleman," sniffed Cerise, surveying the crowd as she sipped her martini.

The DJ for the makeshift disco on the upper deck began his set, Moby's "Go" filtering down and washing over the crowd. Cerise promptly downed her drink and slammed the empty glass on the bar. "Come, we are dancing," she said, heading for the stairs.

Pandora took Ty's hand. "Come, we are dancing."

When Pandora and Ty reached the observation deck people were already streaming onto the dance floor, and Cerise was in the center. It clearly hadn't been her first dirty martini of the evening, but she was no less graceful in her movement, a vision, smoothly in sync with Moby. Ty put his lips to Pandora's ear to be heard over the music. "Georg's wife wasn't loving Cerise," he said, laughing.

"A lot of wives aren't loving Cerise."

"You don't have to worry about me," said Ty.

"I know," she smiled, leading him onto the dance floor to join her friend. "She's had a bad night, that asshole hit her in the face."

"No shit," said Ty. "Probably just as well I didn't know that when he nearly knocked you into the river."

"No shit," she said, "I don't think our hosts would have appreciated you two rolling around the dock in your nice black suits. So be extra nice to her, OK?"

"Hey, I think she's adorable."

Cerise signaled to them to get their asses on the dance floor and Ty followed Pandora over to her, now surrounded by grooving Czechs, Slovaks, Germans, Swedes, Japanese and two Americans. Pandora beamed, Ty was not only dancing, but he actually seemed to be enjoying it. She and Cerise circled him like planets around a sun. They sandwiched him, Cerise in front and Pandora behind, pressing her breasts to his back, then Cerise faced her, dancing closer than Pandora had ever danced with a woman, and combed the hair from her eyes. Pandora flushed, not sure how she felt about it and checked to see if Ty had seen. She suddenly wanted to kiss him hard on the mouth but resisted because she didn't want to make her friend uncomfortable. Then she thought how silly that was, he *was* her husband. But she still didn't kiss him. Then the DJ segued into ABBA's Voulez-Vous, and Panda thought *Shit, Ty hates ABBA.*

Cerise didn't miss a beat but Ty looked suddenly sour. He leaned into Pandora's ear and said, "This guy sucks," referring to the DJ, then, "I just saw a minister I've been trying to get on the phone for three weeks."

"Go ahead," said Panda, disappointed but not surprised.

"You OK?" he checked.

"I'm fine, go. Just be sure you're bearing two fresh martinis when you return."

"No problem," he said and made a beeline for the minister, who was trying to get a bartender's attention.

Cerise leaned in, "Is he OK?" she asked in French.

"He's fine, just ABBAphobic," shouted Pandora over the music, answering her in French as she always did now.

"They are old fashioned," said Cerise.

"And he saw some minister he's been trying to reach," said Pandora. "He'll get us fresh drinks when he's done."

"That will be good, but I have something better," smiled Cerise, displaying a neatly-rolled joint. "Would you like to get high?"

"God, I don't know," said Pandora, "it's been years."

"This is supposed to be amazing, from Thailand," said Cerise. "Come on," she said, taking Pandora's hand and leading her towards the Lady's room. Which, they discovered, was knee deep in women waiting to freshen up.

"No problem," said Cerise, "I know somewhere else."

Cerise led Pandora down to the main deck, then lifted a door to a stairway taking them below. They descended the narrow steps, following a rhythmical chugging sound.

"Are you sure it's OK for us to be down here?" asked Pandora.

"Absolutely," said Cerise, opening a second door and revealing the museum-quality steam engine, resplendent with bright red paint and mirror-finish brass. "At another party the captain himself showed it to me. He was as energetic as this motor."

She pushed Pandora into the cramped space and locked the door behind them. "Just don't touch anything that looks like it will blow us up."

"Oh, that's reassuring," said Pandora.
Cerise opened her purse and brought out the joint and a Cartier lighter.

"My problem is the smoke," said Pandora. "The last time I tried, I coughed like I had emphysema. It kind of wrecked the high."

"No problem," said Cerise, "I know just the thing." She lit the joint, inhaling deeply, then exhaled.

"Here," she said, standing close in front of Pandora. "When I exhale, you inhale." Cerise took a deep hit.

"But—" Pandora started to say but Cerise touched her finger to her lips, stopping her words, then leaned in and blew the smoke into her mouth, their lips barely touching.

Pandora breathed in, then exhaled a cloud of smoke, momentarily light-headed.

"See?" said Cerise.

Pandora wasn't sure what she was supposed to be seeing.

"Was that nice?"

Of course, thought Pandora, *she meant the marijuana was nice. What else would she have meant?*

Cerise took another hit and leaned in to Pandora's mouth, and this time their lips met more firmly as she exhaled, and Pandora took in the sweet smoke. But now Cerise's lips stayed on Pandora's as she exhaled, and Cerise pressed against her, pushing her against the counter behind the huge, pounding engine.

Dizzy, Pandora held that moment for what seemed an eternity, then she felt Cerise's tongue gently probing, its touch promising delights she'd tried to put out of her mind. Pandora settled into Cerise's kiss and her embrace. "Your lips are so soft," she whispered.

"I think you wanted to do this that first day in your shop, no?" answered Cerise.

"I don't know," said Pandora. "I've never done this before."

"I know, I can tell," said Cerise, pressing harder against her. "I want to kiss you someplace else," she said, and Pandora thought how perfect French was for this conversation. "Will it be OK?"

"I think so," said Pandora, a war of emotions raging in her. Cerise kissed her neck and her breasts, her nipples hardening beneath the thin rayon of her dress and the lace of her bra.

Now Cerise dropped to her knees, kissing Pandora's belly through her dress, then lifted its skirt revealing the triangle of her thong covering her perfectly tonsured pussy.

"So pretty," said Cerise as she kissed her thighs, inside and out, more urgently now, kissing Pandora everywhere down there but her pussy, as she stripped the thong from her hips and slid it to her feet.

Oh my God, thought Pandora, running her fingers through her hair, honestly, not knowing what to do with them or what she should do at all. Then they found Cerise's hair and she was holding Cerise's head in her hands as the woman kissed her, kissed her everywhere but her pussy. Pandora nearly tripped, her panties around her ankles, then stepped one foot out of them, still holding Cerise's head tight in her hands and pulled Cerise's mouth to her clit, where the French girl's tongue fulfilled its promise and more.

Now Pandora leaned back over the counter, bracing herself with both hands as Cerise's tongue explored, now pushing itself into her vagina, then returning, wet, to her erect pink clit.

The steady rhythm of the steam engine increased in tempo and power as Pandora's head swam in a river of ecstasy, her hands returning to Cerise's head, pulling her harder into her pussy until her moans rose to a scream in the same moment as the captain sounded the boat's whistle.

Now sensitive, Pandora pushed Cerise away, giggling in the moment. She pulled her to her feet and their lips met again.

"My God, Cerise," whispered Pandora hoarsely.

"I know," said Cerise, and pressed her mouth hard against Pandora's. Pandora pulled her close, crushing their breasts between them and pushing her leg between Cerise's thighs, pulling her skirt up so she felt her pussy pressing against her. Pandora held her tighter, now feeling Cerise's thigh on her pussy and the two moved as one, their muffled breathy moans synchronized with the puffing of the steam engine and the thrusting of their hips until they nearly collapsed in a huge mutual sighing climax.

Still they held each other, quiet now but gently kissing, nibbling at each other's lips.

"I think you've been saving this for a while," said Cerise.

"I don't know, maybe I have," Pandora replied. "We should get back to my husband, he'll think we fell overboard," said Pandora, switching to English.

"We did," said Cerise as she opened her purse and took out a small mirror and her lipstick. She touched Pandora's lips, erasing the lipstick smear. "This color is good on you. Let's try some more." She opened the case and carefully applied it to Pandora's mouth. Pandora closed her eyes dreamily, delighting in her touch.

"You're right, having someone else do your makeup is wonderful," Pandora said.

Cerise gave her a tissue to blot her lips.

"Ready?" she asked.

"Wait," said Pandora, "I have an idea."

Cerise smiled wickedly and combed Pandora's hair with her fingers.

"You want to do it again?"

"Sort of," said Pandora, "but not here, and...well, do you find Ty attractive?"

"Very. I'm sorry his brother is married."

"How would you feel about coming home with us tonight?" ventured Pandora.

"You mean a threesome?"

"If it's too weird, I'll understand."

"Too weird?" laughed Cerise. "You must be joking."

They found Ty at the water-level bar, the same beer half-finished in front of him, along with two dirty martinis. An aggressive slightly drunk young woman with determinedly revealing décolletage was working at holding his attention.

"Ah, here you are," said Ty, hugely relieved to see his wife. "I was afraid you fell in the river."

Pandora gave him an intense territorial kiss, then smiled at the girl. "I don't think that bra does a thing for you, or the dress," she said in Czech. She took her card from her purse and gave it to the girl. "Here's my card, you must come and see me."

The girl looked at it, put it on the bar, and said, "Nice talking to you" to Ty in Czech as she pushed off in pursuit of other game. Pandora picked up one of the martinis and took a sip as Ty looked at her, suddenly alert.

"Funny, I'd swear your mouth tastes like—"

Pandora put her lips to his ear. "Pussy?" she whispered.

"Kind of," he said.

She downed the martini, then leaned back in to his ear and said, "How would you feel about the three of us taking the party to our house?" she whispered.

Ty raised an eyebrow, one of his most endearing qualities, and noticed for the first time that, Cerise was hanging on Pandora's shoulder, curiously close, watching him intently with a little smile on her lips.

"Seriously?" he asked.

"Very," said Pandora and Cerise almost simultaneously.

The boat's whistle sounded as the engine reversed.

"We're about to dock," said Pandora, putting her hand on her favorite part of his anatomy. "Hurry up and decide, this isn't going to suck itself."

"Good point, shall we go, ladies?" He said, placing a firm hand in the small of each of their backs to guide them into the throng departing the boat. As they neared the gangway they shuffled passed the low roof covering the engine room, with its glass skylight offering passengers a view of the polished machinery of the steam engine.

Oh, dear, thought Pandora and nudged Cerise.

"*Mon Dieu*," laughed Cerise. "Perhaps we are famous now?"

Pandora looked around but no one seemed to be giving them any special notice, so any steam engine buffs would seem to have been at the bar for their performance.

§

Ty downshifted his Porsche, the engine howling as he pushed it through the narrow streets, Cerise in the passenger seat and Pandora wedged between them.

"If I were you, I'd slow down, unless you want to see those martinis again," said Pandora.

Ty looked in his rear-view mirror. "Looks like someone agrees with you," he said, pulling over to the curb, the car lit by flashing blue light.

The cop climbed off his motorbike and walked ceremoniously around the car, then leaned in Ty's open window. "Good evening, sir," he said in Czech. "Nice car."

"Thanks," answered Ty in Czech. "Is there a problem?"

The cop had a hungry smile. "There's always a problem, isn't there?" he said, craning for a better look at Pandora's legs.

"Do you want to see my license?" asked Ty as he removed his wallet from his jacket pocket.

"That isn't necessary," said the cop, as he moved on to Cerise's legs. "You are American?"

"Czech/American."

"You speak Czech well. It appears you have your hands full. Who are these ladies?"

"My wife and my," he hesitated, "sister-in-law."

"Have you been drinking?"

"I had a beer. Would you like to test me?"

"That shouldn't be necessary," said the cop, wondering why it was taking Ty so long to give him the bribe.

"Just give him five hundred koruna, so we can get out of here," said Pandora in English, wondering the same thing.

Ty sighed as he pulled the bills from his wallet. "Thanks, officer."

The cop slid the bills into his pocket. "Drive carefully, sir, you have precious cargo."

Ty started the car as the cop returned to his motorbike, five hundred koruna richer.

Pandora looked at Cerise, speaking in French, "My husband is the last honest man."

"Eureka," replied Cerise. She looked over at Ty and smiled, speaking in her charming English, "I feel like this man Diogenes."

"It won't always be like this here," grumbled Ty as he slammed the car in gear and accelerated into the night.

§

Ty closed the door of their townhouse behind Pandora and Cerise, the latter wide-eyed. "It's so beautiful," she said, as Ty took their wraps.

Cerise headed off to explore the living room but Ty held Pandora back. "Are you sure you want to do this?" he whispered. She pulled his lips to hers.

"I'm sure I want *us* to do this," she whispered back. "Champagne!" said Pandora, beckoning Cerise as she headed for the kitchen.

Cerise, stopped, awed, in the doorway to the granite and stainless-steel kitchen. "*Mon Dieu*," she murmured. "This is wonderful."

Pandora opened the refrigerator and brought out a bottle of Veuve Cliquot, took three flutes from a wire rack, popped the cork on the bottle and filled the glasses. She gave Cerise a glass, then they noticed Ty, standing shyly in the doorway.

"What are you waiting for?" said Pandora, "I've never seen you shy."

"I've never seen two such beautiful women," said Ty, picking up his glass.

"Oh," said Cerise in French, "I think this one might be dangerous after all."

"Never underestimate him," said Pandora.

Ty lifted his glass. "To our beautiful new friend," he said, and they clinked their flutes and drank.

Pandora grabbed the bottle and Cerise's hand. "If you like the kitchen, you'll love the bedroom."

Ty followed them up the stairs, wondering at their astonishing butts and the beauty of life, in that order. When he entered the bedroom, the girls were at the window, with its view of the Charles Bridge. He put his glass on the nightstand and turned on the light. Pandora protested. "No light! We want a fire, slave boy."

"And a fire you will have, Madam," said Ty. As he lit the gas fireplace Pandora reclined on the bed with her Champagne and Cerise peered into the expanse of marble and glass of the master bathroom.

"Your *bain* is big as my apartment," she said.

Ty took off his jacket and tie and lay down next to his wife, who refilled his Champagne glass. Seeing this, Cerise finished her wine and knelt on the bed beside them, holding out her glass for more. Pandora refilled it, then her own. This time she toasted them, raising her glass. They clinked and she downed hers, then threw the glass into the fire. Cerise did the same, then the two women looked at Ty, his glass only missing a sip. Under the enormous weight of the peer pressure, he lifted his glass again, drained it and smashed it in the fire.

"All right, Tibor," said Pandora, lying back and pulling him in for an intense kiss. Then, giggling like a schoolgirl, she pulled Cerise over, so she straddled them both. "Time to get serious," she said, finding Cerise's mouth with her own as she traced the woman's curves with her hand. Satisfied she turned Cerise's luscious lips over to Ty, who received the same promise from Cerise's mouth and tongue Pandora got in the steamboat's engine room. Head swimming, he felt an inquiring hand on his cock but for the life of him couldn't guess whose.

Now Cerise returned to Pandora's mouth and Ty kissed her neck, her breast filling his hand. Pandora unzipped Cerise's dress and pulled it over her head, then lifted her up so her bra was in their faces. Cerise unhooked it and Pandora and Ty kissed her breasts, Cerise holding their heads as she pushed her swollen nipples into their mouths. As she sucked on the glorious pinkness, Pandora slid Cerise's thong from her hip and realized she had help from her partner. Thus unencumbered, Cerise continued up and straddled their faces, and Pandora and Ty's tongues entwined with Cerise's urgently beckoning clit. As she pushed her pussy into their mouths, Pandora and Ty held her ass with their hands, encouraging her thrusts. Then Ty licked his fingers and pushed them into her and she cried out, head back, breathing in sync with her rolling hips, just to the edge of climax, where she screamed in frustration and backed down kissing them both.

In no time Pandora's dress was over her head, her bra was off, and Cerise's mouth was on one of her breasts while Ty kissed her neck and bit her shoulder. Then the women turned on him. Not bothering with buttons, they tore his shirt off, then worked together getting his pants open. They pulled them off, then both fell on his huge, rock-hard cock, kissing and licking it, their lips meeting as they slid their mouths over the shaft, its veins bulging.

Ty pulled his wife onto her side beside him, lifted her leg and rubbed his cock against her pussy, pushing the tip between her pussy lips, just enough to wet it, then sliding it against her clit, then back again, a little deeper each time until he had fully entered her, cheered on by Cerise, who was lavishing Pandora's mouth, neck and breasts with kisses.

Now Ty lifted Pandora's leg, spreading her pussy lips to reveal her desperate clit and Cerise descended on it, licking and sucking and biting it in time to Ty's thrusts and Pandora's increasingly urgent moans and cries. And then the mother of all orgasms washed over Pandora, convulsed by a thousand volts of organic ecstasy.

Giggling, the now super-sensitive Pandora pulled Cerise up and the three kissed, tongues intertwined, Cerise sliding her pussy, now wet beyond imagining, on Ty's cock. Desperate, she reached down to take it in but Ty's hand was already there, and he thrust into her so fast and hard she gasped, and he probed till the tip found her cervix, eliciting an anguished moan. Cerise sat upright on him, taking in every millimeter and rocking for more, as Pandora lavished his mouth with kisses.

Now Pandora's mouth found Cerise's thigh, moving up to her belly and breasts to her mouth. She moved behind her, pressing her breasts to her back, thrilled by Cerise's ass rubbing against her as Cerise rocked on Ty's cock. Kissing her neck, Pandora cupped Cerise's breasts, and Cerise leaned her head back to find Pandora's mouth in a mirror image of Pandora's dream.

Now Ty reached for his wife's hand and pulled her around, lifting her ass in the air, pulling her over till she straddled his face, his tongue wetting itself from her pussy lips, then focusing intently on her clit. Pandora smiled, rocking gently on his mouth as Cerise did on his cock. The women leaned in till their mouths met in a soft kiss, completing the connection, and the three moved in unison, a perfectly balanced universe in microcosm. As Pandora felt the approaching wave of her climax she opened her eyes, as did Cerise at that instant and they moved together, eyes and lips locked, hands on each other's hips, until they arrived together, merged as one in the delirium.

As one, both women collapsed on Ty, lavishing him with kisses. Cerise's hand stroked his still hard cock. "But you didn't have orgasm with us, *Monsieur Ty*," she said, "you are still so hard."

Pandora nuzzled her breasts against his face. "He's very polite about waiting his turn," she said in French.

"How sweet," marveled Cerise, speaking French as well.

"Also, he likes to finish in your mouth."

"Is this true?" said Cerise, in mock surprise. "This is so unusual for the man."

"I can understand you, you know," said Ty in English.

"It's OK," said Cerise in English, "I love this."

"He knows I do," said Pandora.

Cerise gestured towards the throbbing cock she gripped in her fist. "Please, after you."

"No," said Pandora, "you're our guest."

"Are you sure?"

"Absolutely," said Pandora, "it's an experience I wouldn't want you to miss."

Without further ado, Cerise planted herself on her knees between Ty's legs and held his cock between her breasts, and he moaned and thrust against her. Now she stroked it, now she rubbed it against her nipples, now she pressed her breasts against it as he fucked them, the swollen tip straining to reach her mouth, which finally complied first with a discreet kiss, then a tongue beneath the tip, until Ty could take no more teasing and forced her head down onto the shaft. Maneuvering for leverage, Cerise pulled his ass into her lap, so her breasts pressed against his balls, and went to work, applying expert suction as the shaft slid in and out of her mouth, first pressing against her throat, then retreating, the tip at her lips, then repeating the process, each time a little faster, a little more intensely.

Pandora's mouth was locked on his and she stroked his head as he writhed and moaned beneath Cerise's expert ministrations. Then she recognized the sound of the approaching storm of his climax. His moans rose to a shaking scream, then a howl and Cerise's eyes popped as he filled her mouth with his cum. Still he screamed as his cock throbbed, each aftershock sending another load against Cerise's throat.

Then as quickly as the storm approached, it passed, and he pulled Cerise up to them, laughing.

"*Mon Dieu*," she said, still swallowing, "he is the wonder."

"I know," laughed Pandora, kissing her and probing her mouth with her tongue. "It might be because of all the dairy."

"And it's so sweet, *non*?" marveled Cerise.

"Pineapple juice," said Pandora, "he drinks it every day."

"What an angel," said Cerise.

They looked at the "angel," now sound asleep.

"In this he is not so unusual," said Cerise.

"Nature's sleeping pill," said Pandora as she gently kissed his forehead. She pulled the blanket up and snuggled into him, pulling Cerise to her back, and they followed him into dreamy sleep.

§

Pandora woke, momentarily disoriented, as morning sun spilled in the bedroom window. Then she remembered it hadn't been a dream and saw that it wasn't Ty curled up against her. She carefully lifted Cerise's arm from her waist and slid out of bed. She found her robe in the closet and was slipping it on when Cerise stretched, then smiled at her from the pillow. "Good morning, my friend. Ty has gone already?"

"He was up at six."

"My God," said Cerise. "But he was quiet like a mouse, no?"

"Just like a mouse," said Pandora. "I need coffee. Can I make some for you as well?"

"Ah, yes, please but first may I take the shower?"

"Help yourself. There are towels, shampoo, everything."

In the kitchen, Pandora ground the coffee and filled the funnel in the espresso machine. Then she looked up thoughtfully toward the bedroom.

As she walked through the bedroom door, she heard the running water and followed the sound to the bathroom, where Cerise stood under the hot rain in the huge glass enclosure, her face turned into the stream. Pandora let her robe fall from her shoulders, opened the door and stepped in. She put her hand on Cerise's shoulder, and the woman smiled, wiping the water from her eyes.

"Allo, belle," said Cerise. She gave Pandora a little kiss on the lips, then another, a little more intensely, and Pandora melted into her embrace, dizzy as she felt their breasts crushed between them and Cerise's thigh pushing between her legs.

Cerise wet the loofah then soaked it with shower gel and gently scrubbed Pandora's neck, then her breasts, lovingly, then her back, pressing their soapy bodies together and kissing her again. Cerise dropped to her knees and scrubbed Pandora's ass and legs, then, very, very gently, her pussy. Pandora sighed, leaning back as the spray hit her face.

"Give me the wand," said Cerise, "this soap doesn't taste so good."

Pandora gave her the sprayer and Cerise rinsed the soap from her pussy. Then, still directing the stream on her most delicate place, she pushed her tongue between her pussy lips until it found Pandora's clit or, rather, Pandora's clit found her tongue. Pandora sighed as Cerise entered her with her fingers, careful not to scratch with her long nails. Pandora held her head in her hands and fucked her mouth, until she cried out, shuddering with pleasure.

She pulled Cerise to her feet and kissed her hard, pressing her against the wall, then kissed her breasts, sliding her hand across her belly and between her legs, and Cerise sighed, "Oh, Pandora."

Pandora slid to her knees, kissing Cerise's thighs, pushing them apart and spreading her pussy lips with her thumbs as she kissed it, sliding her tongue from her clit to her vagina, pushing it in her and Cerise squirmed and moaned. But Pandora's tongue soon returned to Cerise's clit, and she cupped her ass in her hands and pulled her pussy to her mouth, guiding her thrusting hips as she licked and sucked and gently nibbled her until she screamed, nearly slipping and falling.

Cerise pulled her back up to her mouth and they kissed beneath the hot stream. "Now I'd like that coffee," she laughed.

three

Ty, in sweaty tennis whites, was looking into the refrigerator when Pandora shuffled into the kitchen in her robe and slippers.

"Hello you," she said as she wrapped an arm around his neck and pulled him in for a kiss.

"Hello, beautiful," he said. "Our guest still here?"

"She left an hour ago, and I went back to sleep. Disappointed?"

"Nope," he said absently, "I'm glad you're getting some rest." He moved things around in the fridge, making a show of not finding what he was looking for. "I thought we had some fresh pineapple juice."

Pandora pointed to it.

"Cool, thanks," he said, picking it up and letting the door close.

"I'm doing a scientific study on refrigerator blindness," she said as she filled the coffee grinder with nearly black French-roasted coffee beans. "The tragic condition is unique to husbands." She put the lid on the grinder, pressed the button, and the room was filled with the sharp, rich promise of espresso. "I'm thinking there might be Nobel in it."

"It was behind the milk," said Ty defensively, filling a glass. He took a sip.

"It's a foot tall and bright yellow," said Pandora, scooping the aromatic powder into the espresso machine. "How was your tennis match with the infamous Minister of Regional Development?"

"I made sure to win one game a set so he wouldn't suspect."

"When you have your construction permits you can skunk him."

"Now that wouldn't show much gratitude, would it?" said Ty. "By the way, he wants us to have dinner with him and his wife."

"Will it help you with the permits if I bat my eyelashes at the geezer?"

"He's not quite a geezer," said Ty. "In fact, he's quite good looking, and quite a player, which is worrisome, since his wife's insanely jealous."

"That isn't your problem," said Pandora.

"It could be," he said, "another scandal would likely bring on a new government, which would mean I'd be back at the starting line."

"Well, in that case, I'll be as demure as a schoolgirl."

"That would really drive him crazy."

"Did you have breakfast?"

"Yeah, at the club. How was your morning?"

"Lovely," said Pandora. "We had coffee and croissants, then she made me show her every piece of lingerie I have. We wear the same size bra, which I'm sure you noticed. She tried every one of mine on. She wants me to order, like, five of them for her. She's a lingerie-aholic."

"Sorry I missed that."

"There, you are still thinking about her."

"Are you kidding? Last night was astonishing, and you definitely enjoyed it too."

"You're right," she allowed, "I just don't want it to, you know, change things."

"The only thing that changes is I love you more every day," said Ty, taking her in his arms.

"Good answer," she said. She kissed his neck. "Mmm, I like it when you're sweaty and salty, like a big lump of caviar." She slid her hand down the front of his shorts and felt him getting hard, then she whispered in his ear, "I want your big hard cock in my mouth." She fell to her knees, tearing at the button and zipper of his shorts, then pulled them to his ankles, along with his jock and, *voilá*, his big beauty was in her face.

She grasped it in her fist, teasing the tip with her tongue, then slid it between her lips until it pressed on her throat. Still she pushed, taking it into her throat until her nose was pressed against his belly and his balls against her chin. She held it there, savoring the sensation of every centimeter of its throbbing wonderfulness in her mouth and throat, until she had to breathe and withdrew it, stroking it in her fist as she looked up into his eyes.

"God, you have a beautiful cock," she said.

"Shucks, ma'am," he said, light-headed as he braced himself against the center island. Right friendly of you to say that."

She cupped his ass in her hands and took his cock back into her mouth, stroking the length of it with her lips, tongue, and throat but Ty lifted her to her feet, interrupting her work.

"I'm not done," she protested.

"Neither am I," he said, turning her around and lifting her belly-first onto the island. He lifted her robe to her waist and it framed the inviting globes of her ass. He spread her thighs and her pussy glistened; nothing made Pandora wetter than sucking cock. He teased her pussy lips with the tip, wetting it in this most natural manner, then he grabbed her hips and thrust the entirety of it into her, making her gasp, "God, fuck me, Ty, fuck me." And he did, pounding her into the island until she cried out with pleasure that sounded almost like pain.

Still he fucked her, his moans promising his approaching climax, and she twisted out from under him.

"I'm not done," he protested.

"Neither am I," she said, falling to her knees and taking his painfully throbbing cock in her mouth, stroking it with her tight fist until he screamed, his cock gushing cum against her throat like a fire hose. She gulped the first load, knowing more was coming with his aftershocks, and she wasn't disappointed, swallowing each in turn, till he pulled her up to him and held her, his body still quivering.

§

Later they sat on her robe, naked on the floor of the kitchen, his arm around her as they leaned back against the counter.

"I like this view of the kitchen," said Ty.

"Amazing what a difference a small change in perspective makes," said Pandora.

"We haven't spent a Sunday like this in a long time," he said.

"We work so hard to live a certain way, then we don't take the time to actually do it," said Pandora.

"That reminds me," he said, "the minister offered us his country house next weekend."

"Are the minister and Mrs. Minister included in the deal?"

"Just us."

"But the shop."

"Get Mrs. Pinski to watch it," he said.

"It's bad enough she'll be watching it while I'm in Paris. She's so worried someone's going to steal something she follows the customers around like Javert," Pandora said.

"So, it's one extra day, at least you know all the stock will still be there Monday."

"No kidding," said Pandora.

"C'mon, Panda, you know we need this."

§

Pandora leaned her head against the Porsche's headrest and held her scarf out in the wind as Ty pushed the car through the hilly curves.

"About now Mrs. Pinsky is demanding to see what's in someone's handbag," she sighed.

"Stop it or I'll spank you," said Ty.

"Promise?" she smiled.

He slowed as they approached a side road marked by an ancient wooden sign reading Demkakova, and turned onto the road, surrounded by thick pine forest.

"God, smell that air," he said.

"It's wonderful," said Pandora, "you were right, as usual."

"I'd think you'd be used to it by now."

They came out of the woods into a clearing, and there was Minister Demkakova's "house," a twenty-room white, tile-roofed villa, overlooking a lush tree-filled valley, a river cutting through its center.

Ty drove into the circular drive and parked. They were quietly awed for a moment.

"Who says public service doesn't pay?" murmured Pandora.

Ty got their luggage from the back, unlocked the door and pushed it open. "After you, Mrs. Krizova," he said, gesturing grandly.

"Thank you, Tibor, you may take my things to my room while I freshen up," she said, then looked momentarily confused. "If I don't get lost finding the powder room."

They walked through the house, like guests at a museum. It had been grand before the war, and the furniture and velvet wall covering, while worn, was still lovely, reflecting the quality and expense of its construction.

"The Commies kicked them out and some apparatchik set his mistress up here. After the revolution Demkakova sued the government and got it back, along with about six other properties that had belonged to his and his wife's families," Ty said.

They found the master bedroom, and Ty put their suitcases on the 18th-century canopy bed. Pandora threw open the curtains to the balcony and opened the French doors, and took a deep breath. "I'd love to have a place like this someday."

"Think positive thoughts for my project."

"God, I am so thinking positive thoughts about your project," she said. She turned around and looked into the bedroom. "I'm also thinking positive thoughts about what you're going to do to me in that bed."

Ty looked at it dubiously and gave one of the posts a shake. "I'm afraid we'll break it."

Pandora ran in and did a flying leap onto it. "No way," she said, "fat burghers have been fucking their fat wives on this thing for hundreds of years."

"I'm not sure that's the image I want to be focusing on tonight."

But, of course, this wasn't a problem that night when Pandora entered the candle-lit bedroom in the sheer nuisette she'd brought for the occasion. Ty lifted the blankets and she slid in beside him and into his arms, pleased to feel him already hard as she crushed her breasts against his chest and their tongues played a sweet game of tag. He rolled over onto his back, trying to pull her with him so she could straddle him, but she resisted.

"No, it's your turn to be on top," she said as she pulled him back on top of her. "Fuck me hard."

Ty slid above her, reveling in the firmness of her breasts on his chest and his belly sliding on hers. He tested her pussy lips with the tip of his hard cock, wetting it, then slid it against her clit, then back to push it into her a little further, then withdrew, then repeated the process until his cock was wet to its base and buried as deeply in her as physics and geometry would allow.

Resting his full weight on her, he reached down and pulled her legs apart so he could get in deeper, probing and reaching until she gasped, the swollen tip of his cock pushing against her cervix. Pandora screamed, twisting under him as she climaxed. Ty started to pull out, but she stopped him. "No," she said, "finish in my pussy, fill me up with your cum."

Ty attacked her like a madman, thrusting against her with every ounce of his strength. Her head hit the headboard and she pushed pack with both hands as he pounded her into the mattress, howling as he gushed in her.

Ty lay on her, limp as a sleepy two-year-old, as his aftershocks were met by the pussy spasms of her second, quieter orgasm. They kissed, then he rolled off her and pulled her head onto his shoulder.

"Not bad for an old married couple," he said.

"You could say that about the whole week," she replied, kissing him, then jumped out of bed and headed for the bathroom.

"Where are you going?" he asked.

"I need to freshen up, unless you want to sleep with the mother of all wet spots, Cum Boy."

When she returned, she snuggled on his arm.

"I never dreamed we could share that," he said.

"You mean with Cerise? You said you thought about it all the time," said Pandora.

"Thinking about it and expecting it to really happen aren't the same. Are you having second thoughts?"

"Not at all, it was wonderful. I think I learned something about trust. And I know now I'd do anything for you," she said.

"I'd do anything for you, for your happiness," said Ty.

"Anything?" wondered Pandora, as she snuggled into his arm tighter.

"Anything," he said.

"I have a fantasy too," said Pandora.

She let the moment build.

"Well? Tell me. What is it?" said Ty.

"You know how you dreamed of having two women?"

"Uh, yeah," said Ty cautiously, having some idea where this might be going.

"I thought about being with two men once."

"When was this?" he asked.

"It was before we met. I'd forgotten about it."

"How old were you?"

"Sixteen, I think."

"Sixteen? Wow." Pandora was always full of surprises, but he really didn't expect that one.

"I was reading this book, like a, you know, bodice ripper?" she said. "The heroine was on a pirate ship or something and wound up having sex with the captain and his first mate at the same time. That night before I went to sleep, I made myself come thinking about it."

"You imagined getting fucked by pirates?"

"No, two guys from our football team. And in the book she was on all fours with one guy in her pussy and one guy in her mouth, sliding back and forth on their cocks? In my version I was on, like, this coffee table on my back with my head hanging back over the edge of the table. My legs were over one guy's shoulders while he fucked my pussy and the other guy was holding my head while he fucked my mouth all the way into my throat."

"Uh, wow...that's kind of a lot of detail."

"I've always had a really good imagination."

"Did you do anything about it?"

"No, I hadn't even thought about it again until, you know, last week," said Pandora.

"So, is this something you want to do now?" he asked.

"I don't know. How would you feel about it?"

"That is definitely an amazingly hot fantasy. On the other hand, I've never got the attraction of cocks and balls. Don't get me wrong, I'm delighted and grateful you women do, it's just not my thing."

"In other words, it's OK for two women to lick each other's pussies but not for two men to suck each other's cocks."

"I couldn't have said it better even if I were capable of saying the last half of that sentence out loud."

"Isn't that kind of a double standard?"

"You say that like it's a bad thing."

"Whatever, in my fantasy they're just doing me anyway."

Ty was quiet for a moment, and Pandora pushed herself up on one elbow. "Are you OK?"

"I'm all right," he said, decidedly not all right.

"I knew I shouldn't have brought it up," she said. She kissed him and lay her head back on his shoulder. "Forget I mentioned it."

four

Pandora, wearing a blazer over a sheer blouse, short skirt, and heels, sighed as she stood in the aisle by her seat and watched the two expensively suited businessmen glare at each other, each insisting he should be allowed to stow her roll-on suitcase in the overhead. Finally, she offered one of them her briefcase to put up there, which more or less mollified the guy and she was able to settle into her deep leather first class seat. Unfortunately, he and his cologne were in the seat next to her and, more unfortunately, he immediately started working on her in Italian, his little mustache twitching with need.

"I don't understand," Pandora said in Czech, confident he wouldn't hear her American accent.

"English?" he ventured, eyeing her breasts when she wasn't looking directly at him.

"No, sorry," she'd answered as sincerely as possible.

"Francais, Deutsch, Espagnol?" he tried, desperate now.

She shook her head sadly as she slipped on her headphones and leaned her head against the headrest. She heard the door close, and the flight attendant came by checking seatbelts, as delicious aromas wafted from the galley. She loved Air France.

The plane taxied and lifted into the air, then floated over the beautiful city as it turned west. Pandora thought about the events of the previous week. Her biggest concern about their adventure with Cerise had been that it might affect how she and Ty felt about each other. What she hadn't counted on was how it might affect how she felt about herself.

Their weekend had been so wonderfully intense her business trip was almost anticlimactic. She'd even considered postponing it, so hungry was she to make love to Ty again. Old marrieds, indeed. On the other hand, this might be best, to put things in perspective, clear her head. Ty wasn't the only one who'd been surprised by her teenage fantasy, she'd surprised herself talking about it. It clearly made him uncomfortable. Well, best to forget it. Whoever said "What's good for the goose is good for the gander" hadn't had to watch her poor gander fretting over having another guy's naked package in his face.

The seatbelt light went off and the flight attendant came by with Champagne. Pandora took the glass and settled back in her seat. Anyway, since she'd taken this early flight, she could go straight to the showrooms and get everything done in only two days.

§

At Orly, she'd briefly considered saving time by dragging her carry-on around all day but decided it wouldn't take that long to leave it at the hotel, even if it was too early to check in. The cabby had waited while she dropped off her bag and confirmed her room, then took her to her first appointment, which was in an atelier above the retail shop of her favorite line.

A salesgirl greeted her at the door and took her upstairs, where salesmen were showing buyers samples at several tables as rail-thin models moved around the room in various state of undress. Pandora put her briefcase on the receptionist's desk. "I'm Pandora Krizova," she said in French. "I was hoping I could see Giles?" she said, indicating a flamboyantly gay middle-aged man with fresh hair plugs that made his head look like a nailbrush, as he helped out at one of the tables.

"He's running a little late, I think," said the receptionist.

Giles saw Pandora and rushed over to her. "Pandora, my love," he gushed in French, kissing her on each cheek. Pandora averted her eyes from the top of his head, now reminding her of an alien crop circle.

"I'm sorry, Giles," she said, "I should have made an appointment."

"No problem, sweetie, I can take you now," he said, dragging her to an empty table. He pulled beautiful lingerie samples from various shelves and spread them out before her. "You won't believe what we have for you."

"I believe," said Pandora.

The day sped by, with a half-dozen similar meetings, the last one ending after seven. One of her reps had wanted to take her to dinner but she begged off, telling him she had some purchase orders she needed to have done by the next day. Pandora dragged herself back to her hotel and checked in. She was a regular at the small, elegant hotel, so knew there would be a split of excellent Champagne and a basket of fruit waiting for her in her room.

As she got her suitcase and the key to her suite at the hotel desk, two impossibly handsome men got off the elevator, one wearing what looked to be an identical Valentino suit to one of Ty's. They were carrying on a heated conversation in Italian but she caught only a few familiar words. Because they were so beautiful and elegantly dressed, Pandora initially assumed they were gay, but as she wheeled her suitcase to the elevator she was pretty sure they were discussing the size of her tits and the shape of her ass. She smile to herself and thought, *What about my eyes, are they chopped liver?*

In her room, Pandora stored her suitcase on the luggage rack, kicked off her shoes and opened the Champagne. Sipping the Champagne, she hung her blazer in the closet and took off her skirt, neatly draping it over a chair. Then, wearing only her blouse and boy-short panties, she spread the dreadful stack of purchase orders she needed to finish before morning on the bed. She was refilling her glass when the phone rang. It was Ty.

"How was your day?" he asked.

"Crazy, and it's not over. I have about fourteen PO's I need to turn in tomorrow. I'll be up half the night."

"Did you have a nice dinner?"

"I didn't have time. I was about to call room service. How was your meeting with the money?"

"The money loves the project. They're dying to get going. We just need those permits," he said.

"And then we can have a house like Mr. and Mrs. Minister's?"

"It won't hurt," said Ty. "You must be starving. I'll let you call room service."

"OK, I am," she said. "Starving, that is, and I'm scared to even look at the stack of work on my bed."

"No games tonight, I guess."

"Sorry," she said.

"Don't stay up too late."

"Thank you but I have other plans," she sighed.

"Love you, sweet dreams, see you tomorrow."

"Love you."

She hung up the phone and smiled at it for a moment, thinking about how close she always felt to him, even when they were a continent apart. Then she called room service, poured another glass of Champagne, and got down to work. Thirty minutes later her supper came. She checked the hall and saw it was a maid, so let her in without getting dressed. The girl lifted the stainless covers, revealing trout almandine and pale green spears of bittersweet endive wearing a light coating of olive oil and Champagne vinaigrette. A carafe of chardonnay, like liquid gold, sat next to the plate and a steaming pot of coffee. Pandora was anticipating a long night.

§

Pandora worked while she ate but even the coffee couldn't help her concentrate. She looked at the phone again. Ty's "no games tonight" had been a reference to the phone sex they'd enjoyed the last time she'd been in Paris. She poured the last of the Champagne and settled back against her pillows, smiling as she remembered. He'd started by asking what she was wearing.

"Black lace La Mer thong, style #1333, and bra, style #1433, 34C," she'd replied.

"Perhaps we could do without quite such specific information."

"Sorry but you married a lingerie buyer," she smiled.

"OK," he said, "are you touching yourself?"

"Yes."

"What are you thinking about?"

"Your big hard cock in my mouth. What are you thinking about?"

"The exact same thing, by strange coincidence."

"Shocker."

"OK, let's back up," said Ty, "that was too easy. Want to play a game?"

"OK," she said.

"All right, you need a jar of honey."

"I'm in a hotel room."

"Imaginary," he scoffed.

"Oh," she said. "OK, got it."

"Now you blindfold me."

"I like that."

"I thought you would. Am I blindfolded?"

"Yep, totally at my mercy."

"All right, now hide a single dot of honey somewhere on your body."

"Any place in particular?"

"Anywhere I can reach with my lips and tongue."

"Goodness," whispered Pandora.

"Ready?" he asked.

"Ready," said Pandora, already stroking her clit beneath her panties.

"I'm licking behind your ear." Ty's voice was warm over the phone; she imagined his cock hard in his hand as he spoke.

"I love that but there's no honey there," said Pandora.

"All right, I'm trying behind your other ear."

"Nope."

"Am I warm?"

"Not even close," she said.

"OK, my lips are grazing your eyebrows."

"God, I love that, I wish I'd put the honey there."

"I'm kissing your neck, that spot right above your collarbone. Well?"

"Another excellent spot for it. You should have told me you planned on kissing me there."

"Now I'm kissing your breast, all around it until I find your nipple, which I lick until it stands up like a little soldier. I'll just suck on it a little longer, just in case there might be some honey."

Pandora rubbed her palm on her swollen nipple in time to his words. "Sorry, honey, no honey," she whispered hoarsely.

"You're right, that would be so obvious, way too easy. I'll just move a little further south and put my tongue in your belly button."

"The hell you will," she said. Pandora's belly button was insanely ticklish.

"Right," said Ty, "we'll just keep heading south, down to your hip, and thigh, to your knee (stop me if I touch honey) to your foot, which I only kiss on top, not on the terribly ticklish bottom, to your other foot, and back to your knee, and thigh..."

Pandora sighed, her breath coming in little bursts as she played with her clit.

"Wait, I know!" he said. "I'm parting your legs, kissing your inner thighs, back and forth. OK, forth and back, just for good measure. Wait, what's this? Could it be? I'm parting your pussy lips."

Pandora gasped, on the edge of climaxing.

"Just a little kiss, right there."

Pandora had both hands on her pussy now, her breathing faster.

"Now my lips are on your lips, my tongue pushing into you, then sliding up to your clit."

Ty was quiet now, listening to the slight whistle of her rhythmic breathing until she sighed as the soft orgasm washed over her. "Was that nice?" he whispered.

"Lovely," said Pandora.

"So where was it?" he asked.

"Where was what?"

"The honey."

"Oh," she giggled, "I forgot to put it on."

"Cheater," he said, "I could have been looking all night."

Pandora smiled at the memory and looked longingly at the phone, then back at the orders. She sighed, picked up her pen and the next purchase order from the unfinished stack and got back to work.

Three hours later, she woke with a start, momentarily disoriented as she struggled to remember where she was. Scanning the bed and seeing the neat stack of finished PO's she remembered only too well. She shuffled to the bathroom and peed, then dug in her suitcase until she found a small plastic bottle of melatonin and took two. She really needed to sleep. She fluffed the pillows, then sat back on the bed and closed her eyes, waiting for the pills to cut in.

An hour later Pandora woke again, feeling jumpy. She looked at the dinner tray, regretting drinking the coffee. She checked the Champagne bottle but it was empty, as was the wine carafe from her dinner. She tried calling room service and was told they stopped serving at ten but the bar was open till midnight.

She hung up the phone and turned on the TV, channel surfed, then turned it off. She looked at her skirt neatly folded on the chair and her shoes.

§

The bar, warmed by cool jazz, was nearly deserted, with a quiet couple in one corner and a noisy party of drunken Japanese businessmen in another. The bartender looked up from washing glasses as Pandora slid onto a stool. "What can I get you?" he asked in French.

"Champagne, please," she said in kind.

As he took the bottle from the fridge behind the bar she saw the two Italians from the lobby entering, reflected in the mirror behind him. They started for a table but one of them saw her, nudged his friend and they walked over to her.

"*Buona sera, bella,*" he said to Pandora.

"Good evening," said Pandora, in English, understanding his intent, if not his language.

"*Sono Fabrizio,*" he said, then indicated his friend, "*e questo é il mio amico Cristoforo.*"

Pandora extended her hand. "I'm Pandora. I'm sorry but I don't speak Italian."

"*Lei é inglese?*" asked Fabrizio.

"American," said Pandora.

"Ah, American," said Fabrizio. "*Mi dispiace, ma no si parla inglese.*"

"That sounds so pretty but I have no idea what you're saying," she said in English. "Do you speak French?" she added in French.

"*Non, mi dispiace,*" he said, "*no Franch, solo italiano. Possiamo unirli?*" he said, indicating the empty stools beside her.

"Please," said Pandora in English, and they sat down, Fabrizio on her left and Cristoforo on her right.

The bartender leaned in and asked the men in Italian what they'd like to drink. Fabrizio pointed to Pandora's glass, "Champagne." The bartender put two glasses on the bar and filled them from the same bottle he'd used for Pandora's. Fabrizio raised his glass and said, "*Per la donna più bella di Parigi.*" Pandora and Cristoforo lifted theirs, clinked his glass, and the three drank, Pandora already sensing Fabrizio was the more aggressive of the two.

Fabrizio looked over at his friend. "You might as well leave now," he said in Italian, "she is definitely into me." The bartender rolled his eyes. So did Cristoforo, who downed his drink and stood up.

"*Buona notte, è stato bello di fare la vostra conoscenza,*" he said.

"No, please," said Pandora, putting a hand on his arm, "stay, have some more Champagne. I love hearing you talk, even if I don't have a clue what you're saying."

He looked at Fabrizio, who shrugged "whatever" and sat down again. He signaled the bartender, indicating their glasses. "*Un altro, per favore.*"

The bartender refilled their glasses, telling Pandora in French it would have to be the last, since he was closing.

"We'll take a new bottle, then," said Pandora. "Put it on my room," she added, showing him her key.

The bartender didn't even raise an eyebrow as he pulled a fresh bottle from the refrigerator. "Would you like it opened, madam?" he asked.

"No thanks, we'll take it with us," said Pandora.

He put the bottle on the bar in front of her, and she turned to Fabrizio. "He's closing," she said in English, "let's take the bottle to my room." He struggled to understand, then she put a hand on his leg, and he gave Cristoforo a triumphant smile, which evaporated as she placed her other hand on his friend's leg.

She picked up the wine and got down from the stool. "*Allons-y?*" she said, raising an eyebrow.

§

True to form, Cristoforo was polite when they got on the elevator, but Fabrizio made his move as soon as the door closed, kissing Pandora hard on the mouth as he pressed her to him, cupping her breast in his hand. Pandora kissed him back with equal fervor but used the force of his body to press her back against Cristoforo, pushing him into the corner. As Fabrizio's hand explored her body, hers did Cristoforo's, until she found his cock beneath the thin, sleek wool of his suit, and she felt it hardening. Fabrizio's mouth moved to her neck and she leaned her head back and pulled Cristoforo's lips to hers.

The elevator doors opened and they fell out into the hallway, kissing and giggling as Pandora dragged them to her door, where she fumbled with the key as the men teased her with their hands. The bell for the second elevator rang, the doors opened, and an elegantly dressed older couple stepped out, the man holding his room key. Both parties stopped in their tracks and regarded each other. The gentleman cleared his throat and steered his wife in the opposite direction just as Pandora succeeded in opening her door.

Pandora's door flew open and they spilled into the room, the men forcing her against the closet as she discreetly closed the door. She slipped out of their grasp and waved the bottle at them.

"First Champagne," she said in English.

"OK, OK," said Fabrizio grabbing the bottle. She got glasses from the mini bar as he fired the cork against the ceiling, then hurried to her and filled each one. She gave each a glass and they linked arms and emptied them. Pandora smashed hers against the far wall, and they followed suit, then she pulled them to her by their ties, kissing each in turn as she stripped off their coats.

Falling to her knees, she rubbed the rock-hard cocks in their pants, looking up at them wide-eyed and expectantly. No translation necessary, they unbuckled their belts, dropped their pants and shorts, and their cocks stood at attention before her face. She seized one in each fist, stroking them as she looked up at the moaning men, watching their faces carefully.

"*Por favora, Pandora,*" pleaded Fabrizio hoarsely, and she smiled and took the tip of his painfully throbbing cock between her lips and he thrust it hard into her mouth, pushing it against her throat. Applying firm suction she cycled it in and out, while pumping Cristoforo's with her other fist, eliciting moans from both men.

When Fabrizio's telltale breathing and his urgent hands on her head warned her of his impending climax she thought, *Not yet, dear*, and turned her attention to Cristoforo's demanding member, which had at least an inch in length and girth on Fabrizio's, almost as big as Ty's. She looked up at him, dizzy above her, and met his pleading eyes. Still watching his eyes, she put her tongue under the tip, and he moaned, running his fingers through her hair. Now she spread her lips around the tip, tongue still in motion, and he thrust into her mouth, gasping as she let it continue into her throat, taking the entire shaft in until her lips were around the base, her nose against his belly.

"*Mio Dio*," muttered Cristoforo, nearly falling over, and Pandora pulled herself to her feet and kissed them in turn as she unbuttoned their shirts. Their hands fought for the buttons on her blouse, but she stopped them.

"You're not destroying my favorite Armani blouse," she said, carefully undoing the buttons herself.

"*Armani ottimo*!" agreed Fabrizio.

Still in her heels, she slipped out of her skirt and steered them to the coffee table. She carefully unhooked her bra, dropping it on the floor as she lay back on the table, her head hanging off one side.

The men froze for a moment, awed by the vision. Then she pulled Fabrizio to his knees and his cock arced urgently into her mouth, as Cristoforo fell to *his* knees, lifted and spread her legs, and attacked her clit with his tongue. She reached back, grabbing Fabrizio's ass to encourage his thrusts into her throat, then took his cock in her fist, stroking it as she looked down at Cristoforo.

"Fuck me," she pleaded, "I want you inside of me."

Evidently, this language is universal. Cristoforo pulled two cushions from the couch, bringing his cock level with her pussy, which was now thoroughly wet thanks to the mouth fucking Fabrizio had given her, to say nothing of Cristoforo's oral ministrations. He lifted her legs to his shoulders and entered her, she pulled Fabrizio's cock back into her mouth, taking the entire shaft in until it was deep in her throat, and for a moment no one made a sound as the men fiercely fucked her from both ends.

Then the silence was broken as Pandora pushed Fabrizio out so she could breathe, gasping and moaning as Cristoforo continued to plunge into her.

She pulled Fabrizio's cock back into her mouth, holding his ass to guide his thrusts, still taking it in all the way into her throat but allowing her to breathe in the tiny exhalations that signaled the onset of an orgasm, the men matching them with cries and moans of their own. Then Pandora climaxed, screaming, and the sudden grip of her tightening pussy caused Cristoforo to follow her, unleashing a throbbing torrent of cum deep inside her at the precise moment that Fabrizio screamed, pushing into her so she felt the entirety of it throbbing as he released shot after shot of thick cum into her throat.

Fabrizio withdrew his cock from her mouth, and she gasped for air, the three quiet for a moment, in a kind of shock at what had just happened. Then Pandora stood and led them to the bed, lying back and pulling them down to her, kissing them both. Their mouths descended to her breasts and she stroked their hair as they sucked on her burgeoning nipples. Then Fabrizio sighed, settled back on her arm. And he fell fast asleep.

Cristoforo smiled up at her and held a finger to his lips. He helped her carefully withdraw her arm, then lifted her leg and pressed his cock to her still-wet clit. She held his head and their lips met as he entered her again, pushing it in until she gasped in near pain. Then he withdrew it completely, and she sucked on his lower lip as he repeated the cycling, listening carefully to the now familiar sound of her breathing as she built to a climax.

Deep inside her, Cristoforo lingered, exploring with the tip of his cock till he found her cervix, causing her to cry out just enough to wake Fabrizio. "*Non si può scopare Pandora senza me*," he said, with mock outrage. Hard now, he stood up beside the bed and she kissed the bottom of his cock, then took it in her mouth as Cristoforo fucked her harder and harder till he cried out, coming in her again. Exhausted, he rolled onto his back as Pandora lay on her side so she could get serious about sucking and stroking Fabrizio's hard cock.

His cock throbbing, he looked down at her, his fingers in her hair. "*Il mio turno*," he gasped. He pushed her onto her back, and lay down on top of her, forcing her legs apart, and entered her, determined to one-up his friend by giving her the grandest fucking of her life. She wrapped her arms and legs around him, moaning as his thrusts pounded her into the mattress, each one bringing them closer to the brink, until her scream and tightening pussy dragged him over the edge with her.

Fabrizio rolled off her and again all was quiet. To her right, Cristoforo was sleeping blissfully. To her left, Fabrizio was curled up against her, and within seconds was softly snoring. She smiled, satiated, and happily followed them into sleep.

§

Morning's first sunbeam spilling passed the curtains dragged Pandora from sleep. Buried in the pillows, she was momentarily disoriented, then remembered where she was. She hesitated, afraid to move a leg, not only because she wasn't sure which man was on either side of her but out of fear of what surely was the mother of all wet spots. Finally, she reached over but instead of a warm tousled head, her hand felt her briefcase. She pulled the pillow off her head and sat up on one arm. It was her briefcase, the latches open. She lifted the lid and saw the neat stack of completed purchase orders. She looked behind her, but the bed was empty. She looked at the floor in front of the far wall. No broken glasses. In fact, they appeared to be on the shelf above the mini bar, completely intact. Her blazer and blouse were in the closet. Her skirt neatly folded on the chair.

The phone rang. She lifted the receiver, expecting her wake-up call from the front desk. "Hello," she said in French.

"*Bonjour*," said the familiar voice, "this is your seven a.m. wake up kiss," said Ty, following it up with a noisy phone smooch.

"Good morning," she said, stretching.

"Did I beat the front desk?" he asked.

"They're probably calling me now."

"Did you sleep OK?"

She thought about this, then remembered. "I was all jittery from too much coffee and took a melatonin. I have the weirdest dreams when I take it. I'd better get going. I have an early appointment. I'm basically cramming four days into two."

"I'm glad, it means I'll see you tonight. And I have a surprise for you."

"Yeah, what is it?"

"If I told you—"

"It wouldn't be a surprise," she interrupted. "OK, I'll call you from the airport. Love you."

"Love you."

She hung up, gave the room another look, marveling at how real it had all seemed, then took as long a hot shower as time would allow.

Pandora wheeled her suitcase from the elevator into the lobby just as Fabrizio and Cristoforo (were those really their names?) finished checking out. They were already near the door with their suitcases as she reached the front desk. True to form, Fabrizio was doing the talking, only now it was into his mobile phone, so heatedly he didn't notice her tits or ass this time. But Cristoforo gave her a little smile as they passed and she smiled back curiously.

five

The street had been dark for two hours when Pandora's cab dropped her in front of their townhouse. Ty had wanted to pick her up from the airport but when she'd called from Orly, he'd said he was having some work done on the house and it was running later than he anticipated. What this work was, however, was evidently part of his Big Secret.

She smiled to herself as she paid the driver and wheeled her suitcase toward the house. No matter how exhausted she was after a trip like this she still felt girlish excitement thinking about seeing Ty again. Tonight, this was heightened not only by three days of separation but by the lingering memory of the strange dream she'd had her first night in Paris.

Pandora dropped her suitcase by the stairway and followed wonderful cooking smells into the kitchen, where Ty was making salads as two pots steamed behind him on the stove. "Perfect timing," he smiled, taking her in his arms for a hello kiss. She mock-collapsed against him.

"Oh, my God, I really did it to myself this time. I've gone nonstop for three days."

"And it doesn't sound like you slept very well," he said sympathetically. "Do you want to change into something comfy before dinner?"

"Just feed me, I'm starving," she moaned, picking at the salad.

"Post haste. Pandas are cute but dangerous when underfed." He poured her a glass of wine. "However, this might have a calming effect," he said handing it to her. "Sit."

She obediently sat at one of the place settings on the island.

"So, when are you going to tell me this big surprise?" she asked.

"After supper," he said as he drizzled olive oil and vinegar on the salads and put them on the counter.

"Not fair," she said, digging into her salad. "You're taking advantage of my hunger."

"Oh, I haven't begun to do that," he smiled, sitting down to his salad.

After al dente pasta with Ty's peppery homemade red sauce, he refilled her wine glass. "Now it's time for your surprise."

She leaned back, drowsy from the meal. "Do I have to leave this chair?"

"You can start there," he said." He pointed to a tiny video camera near the ceiling in the corner of the room facing the island.

"What am I looking at?" she asked, puzzled.

"It's a video camera," he said, taking her hand. "Come on."

There were two in the living room, one pointed at the sofa and coffee table and one at the fireplace. He led her into their bedroom, pointing out two more near the ceiling in the corners of the room opposite their bed. "There," he said.

She walked over to them and looked up. "Are these in case of burglars?

"Try again."

She looked at the cameras, then at the bed. "Are we making a sex video?"

"One of us might," he said as he directed her to the bathroom, where cameras monitored the shower and tub.

"One of us?" she asked.

He took her to the guest bedroom, where there was a monitor, video recorder, and control board.

"I don't get it. Who's going to be in here?" she said.

"OK, here's the deal," he said. "Thinking about your high school fantasy, and I thought about it a lot, I had to admit it really turned me on. The problem was my own discomfort with being with the other guy while he was, you know."

"Hard?"

"Something like that," he said.

"But why the cameras?"

"So, I can watch you without, you know, being in the action. Anyway, I figure you'd feel safer if I were nearby. I mean, you would, wouldn't you?"

She jumped on him, crushing him in her embrace. "You really do love me," she said, pressing her mouth on his. "It's incredible, you're incredible. But are you sure you can, you know, handle it?"

"That's an interesting way of putting it. Last night I got off three times thinking about it. So you like the idea?"

Suddenly no longer tired, she pulled him onto the bed. "I'm unbelievably turned on. Fuck me, hurry!"

§

When she opened her shop in the morning Pandora wasn't surprised to find that Mrs. Pinsky hadn't made a single sale. But she felt rejuvenated after her Paris trip, and she smiled thinking about how excited their lovemaking had been upon her return. And it was exciting that night, and the next but Ty didn't bring up his "surprise" again that week and she began to think it was just another of the stories and fantasies they teased each other with, which was actually OK, given how inspirational it was. Then Friday night she found herself in one of those bars she'd thought she'd never be in again, a pickup bar packed with hungry-eyed singles, or at least pretend-singles, looking to get laid.

"Are you OK?" Ty asked.

"Sure, are you OK?" She replied, not feeling especially OK.

"Sure," he said, looking a little unsure. All right, if it looks like it's a go, walk out slowly with them so I have time to get to the house and set everything up."

"OK," said Pandora, awed at the situation.

"But if things get weird or uncomfortable, just stick your arms up in the air like you're stretching and I'll come to your rescue."

"They'll think I'm showing off my tits," said Pandora.

"I'm not sure there's anything you can do about that even without stretching. Anyway, if you want out, that's the signal."

Pandora pushed her way through to the bar, standing, since every stool was taken. Immediately the men on either side started hitting on her, one speaking Italian, the other Czech. The bartender leaned over, and she ordered a white wine in Czech. Hearing her accent, the Czech guy switched to broken English, praising her to the moon. His friend, who had been working on a girl on the other side, got wind of her and pushed his way passed the Italian, who was also trying his clumsy English on her. She felt a hand on her ass and turned, expecting to see Ty but it was a fourth man who leaned into her ear and asked her in Czech if she wanted to go for a drive in his "Mercehdess-Banz."

Ty strained to see her, his vision blocked by the mob around his wife. Then both her hands appeared above the crowd.

In the car Pandora was laughing, in spite of how ludicrous it had been. "When I stretched, the Italian grabbed one of my boobs. It's a fun fantasy. Maybe we should leave it at that."

"I'll do whatever you want, Panda," he said.

"Well, right now I want you to fuck me, so either get us home faster or find a quiet spot where I can suck your cock," she said, surprised herself at how excited she was.

"I don't think it will help with my permits if we get arrested," said Ty, downshifting the Porsche and chirping the tires.

§

Ty woke her twice that night; there was no question their fantasy had improved their sex life, which by normal standards was already just fine. She was thinking about this the next morning as the UPS guy, wearing the ubiquitous brown shorts and shirt, wheeled in the boxes stacked on his hand truck.

"What do you have for me, Jarda?" Pandora said brightly in Czech.

"More stuff I don't want my wife to know about," he said, putting the boxes on the floor.

Pandora held up a lacy negligée. "You mean you wouldn't like to see her in this?"

"At this point in the marriage, the more clothes the better," he said, handing her the clipboard for her signature. As he wheeled his hand truck to the door Cerise came in, pausing to hold the door for him. He was appreciative in more ways than one. He'd confided to Pandora on several occasions her shop was his favorite stop on his route because of the scenery.

"*Bonjour Panda*," said Cerise.

"*Bonjour Cerise*," said Pandora, continuing in French. "You always arrive just in time for my new shipments."

"The early bird gets worms," said Cerise in English, nearly getting it right.

Pandora said, "You might want to rephrase that," but Cerise was already shopping.

"This should be what I ordered last week in Paris from my favorite new designer," said Pandora, wisely sticking to French as she opened the first box. She pulled out a tissue-wrapped merry widow and Cerise grabbed it from her hands, purring as she headed for the dressing room, "I have never seen something so beautiful."

A moment later her voice came from behind the curtain (Pandora had finally managed to get her to close it, saying she was going to give the UPS driver a stroke and/or ruin his marriage), "Panda, can you help me? I'm afraid I don't understand this."

As Pandora squeezed into the dressing room, Cerise turned from the mirror to face her. The lacing was hook-and-eye and she'd mismatched the hooks. "These need to match," Pandora said as she unlaced her, releasing Cerise's firm full breasts, her nipples swelling like ripe cherries.

"My breasts always get so swollen and tender this time of the month," she said, combing her fingers through Pandora's hair. "I wish you would kiss them," she said, pouting.

"It's tempting but I think I need to draw the line at having sex with my customers while I'm at work," said Pandora, relacing her firmly.

"I should probably use this rule also," sighed Cerise, as Pandora cinched her up, causing her breasts to explode from the top of the Victorian undergarment like ripe cantaloupes. "Although maybe just as the guideline."

"There," said Pandora, "how's that?"

Cerise turned to the mirror, studying the effect from every angle. "Yes, this is very good," she said.

"Very good doesn't begin to describe it. If your fans don't climb over each other to get to you, check their pulses and call 911," said Pandora, returning to her boxes.

"What is 911?" asked Cerise as she unlaced the corset.

"It means, like, the paramedics?"

"Ah, yes, you're right. I had this problem once, an older Japanese gentleman who was, I think, a little too excited. But his friends insisted on taking him away. It can be very delicate." Cerise came out of the dressing room and put the corset on the counter. "How much will this be?"

"I don't know," said Pandora, "I'll need to check the invoice." She dug in the box until she found it, then entered the amount into her calculator. "Sixteen-thousand koruna," she said.

"*Mon Dieu,*" muttered Cerise, holding it up and looking at it with new respect. "*Tres cher, non?*"

"How's fifteen thousand, for my best customer?" said Pandora.

"Fifteen thousand is excellent," said Cerise, opening her purse.

Pandora looked at her thoughtfully. "It just occurred to me that when you have a problem you ask an expert. Can I have a favor?"

"*Bien sûr, chérie,*" smiled Cerise.

"Ty and I want to go to a party, a really nice one, like the one you invited us to before but where we wouldn't see anyone we know," said Pandora.

"Why does it matter?"

"I'd rather not say."

Cerise put a hand to her cheek. "Horrors," she said, "I've created a Pandastein."

§

The moment Ty parked his Porsche in the drive of the villa a uniformed valet opened Pandora's door and she swung her long legs out, revealing four-inch fuck-me pumps and a good deal of thigh barely covered by the littlest little black dress she could find. Ty gave his keys to a second valet and took his wife's arm. Together, they looked up at the grand doors opening to a brilliantly lit foyer.

"Ready?" he asked.

"Ready," she answered.

A liveried butler took Pandora's wrap as they entered, and they followed the buzz of conversation to a large room with a huge fireplace and clusters of elegantly garbed tipplers, where one of the bars set up in nearly every room was doing a brisk business. A waiter walked by with a tray of Champagne and Pandora took one. "I think I need something a little stronger," said Ty, putting his hand on the small of her back. "If you need me you know the signal."

Ty went exploring. Under normal circumstances, this would be the ideal scene for networking, but he was pleased there were no familiar faces. He found another bar in the drawing room and ordered a Scotch rocks. Ty scanned the room as the bartender got his drink and placed it on the bar. As he stuffed a few koruna in the tip glass and took a sip, an extraordinarily beautiful woman made her way over and put her hand on the bar next to him, an unlit cigarette in her fingers.

"Do you have a light?" she asked in Czech.

"Sorry, I don't smoke," he answered.

"No problem, I just quit," she said, tossing the cigarette over her shoulder. She took a sip of his Scotch. "Are you an American?"

Ty knew he had a slight accent but was always a little surprised when the Czechs were on to him so quickly.

"Yes."

"Your Czech is very good."

"Not good enough, evidently."

"I have a very good ear," she smiled.

"I was born here but we moved to the US when I was a boy."

"Are you one of the Contessa's friends or Honza's?"

"Ah...mutual friend. What about you?" Ty said.

"Beatrice. Believe me, none of Michal's girlfriends will be showing their faces tonight. Her majesty would not be amused."

Ty had no idea what she was talking about. He surveyed the room again and smiled to himself at the thought of the soap opera going on under his nose.

"So why haven't we met before?" she purred. "I thought I'd met all the most handsome men in Prague."

§

Meanwhile, Pandora was nearly surrounded by new admirers, three beautifully tailored young men, Mathias, Alois, and Jakub. They were variously struggling to communicate with this insanely attractive woman who had identified herself as non-Czech-speaking French, a language only Jakub spoke. They finally settled on English, which none of them spoke well enough to recognize Pandora's French-accented English as suspect. Seeing her Champagne flute close to empty, Jakub snagged her another from a passing waiter. "You look so familiar. Were you in Ibiza last winter?" he asked in his Czech-accented French as he gave her a fresh glass of wine.

"Sorry, no," Pandora answered in French, "I've never been in Spain."

"I'd love to take you there," he said, struggling not to stare at her breasts, which Pandora had expertly sculpted with her best bra.

"What are you do, Miss Amabella?" said Alois, using the name Pandora had given them.

"Please, 'Vanessa'," said Pandora, allowing Jakub plenty of time to scrutinize her chest.

"Vanessa, the beautiful name," said Mathias in English, raising his glass, "for the most beautiful woman in Prague."

"Kubie!" The countess' voice rang out from the doorway. Pandora recognized the undeniably beautiful woman's dress as last year's Versace. "I've been looking all over for you," she said, speaking in Austrian-accented Czech as she took Jakub's arm. "Are you going to introduce me to the person who's monopolizing my party's three most eligible bachelors?"

"Of course," said Jakub, politely switching from Czech to French. "This is Vanessa Amabella, a Parisienne who is visiting us on some mysterious business." He turned to Pandora. "This is the Countess Beatrice von Aachental."

"Enchanté," said Pandora, extending her hand. The countess took it like it was a dog turd.

"Charmed, I'm sure," said the countess, her Parisian French flawless. "I'm sure you're having the most fascinating chat but I confess I just came to steal Kubie away from you."

Pandora was relieved to see her lead Jakub away. Her French was very good and, indeed, Parisian but still the woman might hear a slight American accent. "Who is that dreadful woman?" the countess asked Jacob, loud enough for Vanessa to hear.

"What a charmer," Vanessa said in English to the remaining men.

"What is 'charmer'?" asked Alois.

"Another word for cunt," said Pandora.

"Cunt?" said Alois, now completely lost. Swaying slightly from the six glasses of Champagne he'd already had, he snagged three more glasses for them from a passing waiter.

"It doesn't matter," said Pandora. She lowered her voice, addressing them both. "May I speak frankly with you?"

"Of course," said Mathias. "Is all OK?"

"All is very OK," said Pandora. "It's just...I'm not sure how to put this but I find you both extremely attractive and would like to take our little party to a more private spot."

"You mean the *three* of us?" said Alois, wide-eyed.

"Exactly," said Pandora. "Would this be uncomfortable for you?"

"Not for me," gushed Alois.

"Not for me also," said Mathias, awed by the opportunity that had reared its head at what he had expected to be an otherwise routine gathering of the countess' rich, snotty sycophants. "But our hostess would not be approving for us to do something like this in one of her rooms."

"Someone lent me his townhouse for my visit here. But your friend should not be driving now, are you up to it?"

"No problem, I can drive us like the wizard!" he said, slurring his words slightly, which made Pandora wonder if it should be she who does the driving.

Ty, still nursing his Scotch, had found a quiet corner after convincing the predatory woman to seek other game. She was obviously not used to having men say no to her but took it graciously. He finished his drink and turned to the nearest bar for another. As he waited, he checked his watch and a pretty girl smiled at him. "Are we really so boring?" she asked in Czech.

"Not at all, I'm expecting someone," he said, then saw Pandora pass the door with Mathias and Alois in tow. "Excuse me." He went to the door in time to see her request her wrap from a servant. He caught her eye, and she gave him a subtle thumbs-up. As he passed them on his way out, he heard them discussing Pandora in graphic Czech.

"My God, the tits." said Alois.

"The ass," said Mathias.

"She's on fire."

"I want to be first."

"We'll toss for it."

"Oh, very well."

The valet brought Ty's Porsche around just as Pandora came out with her new friends. Ty tipped him, then roared away. They had agreed that she would take a roundabout route to the house but he wanted to be sure to beat them there.

He had nearly reached the house when a familiar blue light lit his rearview mirror. He pulled over to the curb and banged his head against the headrest as the officer dismounted his motorbike and walked around the Porsche to Ty's window. Ty rolled it down and looked up to see it was the same cop. "We have to stop meeting like this," Ty said in Czech, as he took out his wallet and gave the guy five hundred koruna.

The cop counted it and shook his head. "Sorry, it's double for repeat offenders."

§

Despite the delay, Ty still managed to beat them to the house. He set the lights in each room, then opened a bottle of wine and took it to the guest bedroom. He switched on the monitor, put a fresh tape in the VCR, then sat down to test each camera. The light level in the kitchen was too bright, the level in the living room too dim. He adjusted both, then returned to the guest bedroom, locking the door behind himself just as he heard a car in front of the house. From the window, he saw Mathias' Jaguar park in front of his Porsche, then Pandora and the men got out of the car.

Pandora let them in, and the men were on her immediately, Alois behind her, holding her breasts and kissing her neck, and Mathias in front, pressing his hard cock to her leg as he kissed her face and mouth. "Champagne!" she said as she wriggled free. Dropping her wrap in a chair, she headed to the kitchen, leaving the men to stagger into the living room.

"My God, can you believe this?" said Alois in Czech.

"Jesus, no, I'm pinching myself," said Mathias. He brought a coin out of his pocket, flipped it in the air and covered it on the back of his hand. "Call it for firsties."

"Heads," said Alois, not knowing how prescient his call was.

"Sorry, tails," said Mathias, uncovering the coin. He slipped it back in his pocket as Pandora came out of the kitchen with a bottle of Veuve Cliquot and three Champagne flutes.

"Will you do the honors?" she said in heavily French- inflected English as she gave the bottle to Alois, then started the gas fireplace. Mathias pushed the cork off, arcing it across the room, and filled their glasses. They picked them up and lifted them. "*À la passion*," said Pandora as they toasted and drank. The men drained their glasses, then prepared to throw them into the fire. "No," said Pandora, almost letting her French accent drop, "they're Riedel!" This meant nothing to them, but they got the idea and placed them carefully next to Pandora's on a side table.

Pandora pushed them onto the couch, then pulled her dress over her head and stood over them in her black lace bra, thong, and heels, and the men stared up at her goggled eyed, like little boys watching the brilliant light in a Spielberg film. She put a knee between each of their legs and took off her bra, smiling up at the camera in the corner of the room as she untied their bow ties and they ran their hands over her body.

"Take off your coats and stay awhile," she murmured, cat-like, as she pushed their jackets off their shoulders. Hurriedly they unbuttoned their shirts, their hot breath on her breasts.

Sliding to her knees, she undid Alois' buckle and zipper, then Mathias'. After helping them pull off their trousers and shorts, she was face-to-face with a dynamic duo of rock-hard cocks.

Seizing one in each hand, she started stroking them and they moaned, still uncertain of the protocol. Helpfully, Pandora rose up and pressed Alois' cock between her breasts, causing Mathias no end of anguish. Desperate to have her suck it, Alois held her head with both hands and forced it down until he felt her lips on it. Still he pulled her in until he felt it on the back of her throat, then, to his amazement, she took it into her throat until her lips were at its base, her nose against his belly.

Ever the perfect hostess, Pandora found Mathias' cock with her free hand, stroking it as her head bounced on Alois' throbbing member. Then she lifted her head and smiled at them, holding their cocks firmly in her tight fists.

"There's something I've wanted to do for the longest time," she smiled.

The men's minds reeled at the prospect as she sat on the edge of the coffee table and pulled them to their feet, placing both cocks in her face. She sucked each of them politely, then directed Alois to the other side of the table, directly behind her and lay back with her head hanging off the table. A man of no little imagination, Alois understood immediately what was expected of him and in a flash was on his knees, his cock in her mouth and her breasts in his hands.

Mathias too needed no printed instructions. He dropped to his knees, stripped off her thong and spread her legs, pausing to marvel at the beauty of it all for only a moment before he parted her pussy lips with his thumbs and pressed his tongue against her clit, sending electric shocks through her body as she held Alois' hips, encouraging his thrusts into her mouth.

As was previously noted, nothing made Pandora wetter than sucking cock, and Mathias' expert cunnilingus, delightful as it was, made her desperate to be fucked. She pushed Alois free of her mouth, stroking it so as not to lose a millimeter of hardness and looked down at Mathias desperately. "Fuck me!" she screamed, "I want it in me!" Obligingly, Mathias straightened up, lifting her legs to his shoulders and pushed his cock into her so fast and hard she gasped.

Now Alois' cock found her mouth again and the two men fucked her in a frenzy, and she climaxed once and then again as they pounded her, moaning and screaming until Alois shook spasmodically, howling as he shot a huge load of cum in her mouth, followed by Mathias in her pussy, gripping her thighs so as not to topple over. The three hovered there, locked in their symmetrical embrace as a second orgasm washed over Pandora like a warm tropical wave.

Both men collapsed, out of breath, giggling nervously, as Pandora mugged for the camera, pouting her lips in a kiss. Abruptly she sat up and grabbed Mathias' hand. "Let's take the party upstairs." She dragged him to his feet and led him toward the stairs but stopped and looked back at Alois expectantly.

"Me too?" he asked meekly.

§

In the guest room, Ty sat in front of the monitor in his robe stroking his cock as he watched them leave the living room, a pile of spent tissues on the floor beside him. He switched the view to the bedroom cameras, splitting the screen. Pandora walked into view on one of the cameras and lit the gas fireplace, one of the men laying his hard cock in the cleavage of her butt and grabbing her breasts as she bent over. The other man, the one with the larger cock, roughly the size of his own, whom Pandora had predictably chosen for mouth position on the coffee table, appeared on the second screen, which had the best view of the bed.

Then Pandora broke free of the first gentleman's hold and leaped onto the bed, positioning herself on all fours facing the second guy. She reached out to him, pulling him closer and sucking his partially hard cock to full erection again as he stood at the edge of the bed, his hands on her head. Ty switched to full screen on that camera view as he stroked his cock faster.

Faced with the vision of Pandora's heart-shaped ass as she sucked Alois' cock, Mathias, who had been obsessing over her breasts since he'd first seen her at the party, had a new object of desire. He positioned himself behind her on his knees and entered her from behind, gripping the twin globes with his hands. Pandora pushed back against him, feeling the tip deep inside her, at the same time pushing Alois away enough so the tip of his now rigid cock was at the tip of her tongue, then slid it back into her throat, pulling away from Mathias until she held the tip of his cock with her pussy lips, then repeated the motion, sliding back and forth on their cocks.

With the men frozen in the moment, Pandora repeated the cycle a dozen times, loving the huge throbbing cock in her mouth and Mathias' balls slapping her clit when she slammed back against him, until she sensed from Alois' moans and difficulty remaining upright that he was on the verge. She twisted away from the men, pulling Alois onto his back on the bed. Straddling him, she inserted his cock and lowered herself fully on it, spreading her legs wide and straight until it felt as if the tip of the cock deep inside her was nearly level with her navel.   Gasping with pleasure nearing pain, she fell forward onto his chest, kissing him as she rolled her hips on his tumescent probe. Mathias knelt behind her and slid his cock in her butt cleavage, wet from his cum. Marveling at the primal joy of her shape, he outlined her breasts and waist and hips, especially her hips, while Pandora, building to her own verge, moaned, seriously fucking the man beneath her, who was trying to concentrate on the week's soccer preliminary games so as not to come prematurely.

Pandora's undulating, slippery wet ass cleavage felt marvelous on Mathias' cock and, suddenly inspired, he pressed the tip of his aching member against her pink flower, and she stopped her motion, surprised at this turn of events, holding her breath as she felt it slip past her tight sphincter, then push in, and she cried out as it filled her like she'd never been filled before. She hesitated, savoring the unfamiliar sensation of the dueling cocks inside her, a sensation on the cusp of pleasure and pain, then the men took over, thrusting into her in sync, their every motion bringing her closer to the edge of a cliff overlooking a vast warm sea, until she screamed, subsumed by an orgasm so intense she convulsed, her pussy and sphincter seizing on the exploding cocks inside her as the men followed her into momentary oblivion.

The desperate rutting cries of their nearly simultaneous orgasms carried through the walls to where Ty, eyes glued to the monitor and his bare cock in his fist, shook with the fury of a (silent) raging climax, ejaculating an arc of cum onto the screen. All was still for a moment, then the three players on the monitor collapsed onto the bed in a heap.

After a moment of quiet reflection, Pandora pulled free and sat up. Both men were sound asleep. She looked up at the camera and shrugged, then slid out of the bed and signaled mischievously for Ty to follow her to the bathroom, carefully closing the door behind her.

Ty switched the monitor view to the bathroom as she entered and turned on the water in the shower. When the stream started steaming, she stepped into the hot rain and turned to face the video eye near the ceiling, watching her every move.

She wet her hair, the water streaming down her face, then shampooed it, the suds spilling onto her shoulders and breasts. She rinsed, then squirted shower gel on a loofah and began slowly and delightfully scrubbed herself. The serious work over, she returned to her breasts and her pussy. Dropping the loofah, her fingers found her clit, slippery with gel and she closed her eyes and leaned back in the corner, massaging a soapy breast with one hand while she touched herself delightfully, her little puffs of breath indicating the nearness of her self-inflicted orgasm.

Now she had two hands there, one spreading her pussy lips, the other rubbing her clit, and she shuddered and sighed, then opened her eyes and smiled for the camera as she removed the wand from its holder and lavishly rinsed every inch of her body with the warm stream.

She turned off the water, lifted the thick cotton towel from its warming rack and slowly and carefully dried her hair, then her breasts and back and legs and pussy. Then she wrapped her hair in the towel, slid her kimono on and slipped quietly out of the room, blowing the camera a kiss as she opened the door.

In the bedroom the men were sleeping like big babies, their backs to each other. She quietly and carefully spread a quilt over them, turned off the gas in the fireplace and slipped out, turning off the light.

Ty was no longer stroking his cock when he heard the light tap at the door, but it was still hard, so when he unlocked the door to let Pandora in, it protruded prominently from the front of his robe. She burst into the room, quickly closing the door behind her and pulled his lips to hers. Kissing him she felt his cock pressing against her leg and took it in her hand. "It looks like you waited for me," she murmured, biting his lower lip.

"Well," he shrugged, nodding his head toward the pile of tissues by the chair and the video monitor, "more or less."

"It appears you enjoyed the show," said Pandora.

"Almost as much as you enjoyed putting it on."

They looked at the men in the monitor, sleeping in the dark room.

"You wore them out," said Ty.

"It seems to be a universal problem," she said, falling to her knees, "but you're awake," and she took his cock in her mouth, sucking it as she pushed him onto the bed and stripped off his robe. He pulled her up to him, sliding back until he was full length on the bed and she straddled him.

"No," she said, rolling off and pulling him onto her, "I want you on top of me."

Done properly, Pandora found the so-called missionary position supremely satisfying, and Ty knew how to do it properly, finding her clit with his pubic bone as she spread her legs into the flat split she'd perfected in junior high school gym, not knowing how valuable it would be later in life. They moved together thusly, delightfully, for the longest time, until Ty heard her little puffs of breath and gasp and felt the tightening of her pussy muscles and allowed himself the luxury of joining her in a mutual orgasm that was neither convulsive, nor earth-shaking but kitten soft and loving and very sweet.

He tucked his nose into her neck, kissing it as she stroked his back, then his breathing became rhythmic and his body slack, his full weight pressing her into the mattress. Gently, she rolled him onto his side, pulled a blanket over them and snuggled into his dreamy embrace, making perfect spoons.

§

Pandora woke as the morning sun warmed the room and kissed her husband without waking him. Then she remembered where they were, and who else was there as well. She sat up and looked at the monitor. Both men were still dead asleep. Ty woke and stretched, then pulled her back.

"I think there's something I need to deal with first," she said.

"Oh, right," he remembered. He looked at the monitor. "Our guests. It's OK, my dick feels like it's been sandpapered."

"I didn't do it."

"Well, not directly. But you're right, I have only myself to blame."

"You should have used some lotion."

"What can I say? I'm out of practice, spoiled by all that natural lubricant I've been getting for the last five years."

Pandora got out of bed and pulled on her kimono.

"What are you going to do?" he asked. "I mean, you're not going to...you know."

"No, gross," she laughed, "we're done here. I'll just be sending them on their merry way."

She slipped out and Ty sat down in front of the monitor, switching to split screen so he wouldn't miss a thing. A moment later Pandora entered the frame, waved cheerfully to the camera, then shook Mathias' bare foot protruding from the quilt. He woke and stretched, then reached for her.

"Come back to bed, I have a big surprise for you," he smiled.

"After last night it won't be much of a surprise," she said, pouring on the French accent.

"Well come back anyway," said Mathias.

Alois, his hangover crippling, squinted into the bright light then covered his head with the pillow, mumbling in Czech, "You can have her all to yourself this time."

"See?" said Mathias, "it will just be us now."

"I'd love to play some more," said Pandora, "but my husband just called. He was supposed to be in Chechnya two more days dealing with 'family' matters but it appears he took an earlier flight. He's on his way here now from the airport."

"What's that?" said Alois, sitting up abruptly.

"I'm so sorry, I'd like to make us a nice breakfast, and I realize it's inconvenient but he has the nastiest temper and it will be much more inconvenient if he kills us all."

Ty heard the Jaguar starting up in the street below and got to the window just in time to see it roar away, tires squealing as they tore at the cobblestones.

§

Ty sat at the island reading the *International Herald Tribune* as the espresso maker finished gurgling on the stove. Pandora, still in her kimono, poured the thick black liquid into Ty's cup. Then she took the hot dinner plate with sausage and hash-browns from the warming oven, scraped buttery scrambled eggs onto it from the omelet pan and put it in front of him. "None for you?" he asked.

"Maybe some toast in a minute. I have a cruel wine head," she said as she filled her coffee cup.

He let her quietly watch him eat, and then finally brought up the eight-hundred-pound gorilla in the room, the previous night's festivities. "So," he ventured, "you seemed to really enjoy...you know, last night." He took another bite of eggs. "It pretty much looked like your high school fantasy."

"One of them."

"*One* of them?" said Ty, raising an eyebrow.

"I assumed you meant the one we, you know, talked about. I think I covered all of them, actually."

"You seemed quite thorough."

"Are you OK?" she said, putting down her coffee.

"Absolutely. Hey, I got off on it too, literally, about eight times."

"You're sure? There's nothing you want to talk about, I mean, you know, related to what happened last night?"

"No. Well, OK, maybe I just wonder if you, if it's something you want to do a lot of. I mean, you *really* seemed to like it."

"Not at all. It was fun, a fantasy come true. But it's totally out of my system. What about you? What about, you know, what we did with Cerise? Is that totally out of your system?"

"It wasn't in my system in the first place. I mean, I'd done it before. For me, it was more about sharing the experience with you."

"So you wouldn't want to do it again?" Pandora asked as she put a slice of bread in the toaster, her back to him.

Ty took a sip of coffee, thinking about this. "I guess so. I mean, not, you know, on a regular basis, or anything but it would be fun to think it might happen again."

Pandora smiled as her toast popped up.

six

If Pandora's biggest concern about their sexual adventures had been that they not have a deleterious effect on her marriage, the effect was quite the opposite. Ty had wanted sex morning and night, or rather night and morning with the occasional in-between thrown in. A Sunday walk in the woods had even resulted in her getting fucked against a huge beech tree. What she hadn't anticipated was their effect on her. More than once when helping a customer in the tiny dressing room, she'd found herself thinking wistfully of kissing the ripe breasts exploding out of a push-up bra or feeling the bee-stung lipstick-clad mouth on her pussy. And not only had she nearly dropped her coffee when, while waiting to cross the street, she'd been able to make out the substantial tip of a distressingly handsome young man's cock disturbingly far down the leg of his tight jeans, she fantasized about taking it in her mouth later that morning. But, she decided, these were symptoms of overwork and stress and resolved to do something about both.

The doorbell announced the arrival of Jarda, his hand truck teetering with boxes, as Pandora called Ty's office. Mara, his secretary, answered and put her on Musak while she checked to see if he was available. As Pandora signed the UPS driver's clipboard she thought absently about Mara. She was older, at least late forties but had a still astonishing figure. Pandora had certified this close up, as Mara had been in the shop several times. She'd teased Ty about this, causing him to swear in the most adorably indignant manner that wasn't why he'd hired her. Still, she'd wondered more than once what went on at the office. And why wasn't Mara married? *Perhaps she didn't like men...*

Mara came back on the line, "Mr. Krizova's call is running longer than I thought. He's talking with his brother in New York. Do you still want to hold?"

"It's OK," said Pandora, "nothing urgent. Tell him he can call me later or I'll see him at dinner." She hung up knowing Ty's call was probably a difficult one. Tomáš' marriage had been rocky for the last year and Ty had been spending a lot of time talking his brother down from the ledge. As she picked up a box to take to the stockroom the doorbell dinged. Barely glancing at the two women who entered she spoke in Czech, "Welcome to Pandora's Box. If you need anything just let me know." A familiar icy voice answered her in French.

"Well, if it isn't Cinderella, home from the ball."

Surprised, Pandora stopped short of the stockroom door and looked back. It was the Countess Beatrice von Aachental and one of her Euro-trash girlfriends.

"I'm sorry, I don't speak French," said Pandora, again in Czech.

"Really?" said the countess in Czech, "Vanessa, is it? I'd swear Kubie said you were Parisienne. But from your Czech I'm thinking you must be English or American."

"American," said Pandora in English. "But I don't know anyone named Kubie."

"Of course you don't, since I rescued him from your talons before you could drag him off along with my other friends," the countess said, her voice dripping venom. "God knows what you did with them. They wouldn't say but they both seem thoroughly embarrassed by the matter."

"I'm sorry but I have no idea what you're talking about. Now, if you'll excuse me, I have work to do" said Pandora as she continued to the stockroom. "The dressing room is through that curtain, if there's anything you'd like to try."

"No thanks, we're not interested in counterfeit garbage," sneered the countess. She looked at her friend, speaking in German, "Let's get out of her before we step in something."

Shocked, Pandora watched them leave. *Well*, she thought, *it could have been worse. At least the men had been gentlemen about it.* On the other hand, she'd clearly called this viperous creature correctly when she defined "charmer" for Alois.

§

Ty was reading in bed when Pandora came out of the bathroom, dropped her robe and slid under the bedclothes. "I called you at work today," she said.

"I know, I'm sorry. I had this gruesome call from Tomáš and meant to call you after but then Václav showed up with all these papers for me to sign, except they weren't in order and I made him rework all the numbers, and—"

"It's OK," she interrupted. "I told Mara it wasn't anything urgent. I just kind of made a couple of decisions today."

"Really," he said, suddenly interested.

"Really. Seriously, I've been thinking about what you said, about how we work so hard to live a certain way and then wind up not even knowing we're alive. And it's not just the work; it's the stress that comes with it. I want to go somewhere, the Mediterranean, the Caribbean, Brazil, the South Pacific, anywhere there's blue water, no lingerie, permits, UPS or ministers of development, just you and me."

"What about the shop? You hate leaving it with Mrs. Pinski for even three days."

"That's my other decision. I've decided to get some help, to hire someone full time."

"Wow," said Ty, putting down his book. "You mean my little control freak might actually trust someone with her baby?"

"I just feel like I'm missing out on so much, missing out on you, like it's time to stop thinking about it and start living."

"You're preaching to the choir," said Ty.

She ran her fingers through his hair and pulled his mouth to hers. "I've never made love to a whole choir before."

"Well, if anybody can do it, honey, it would be you," he said, switching off the light.

§

Pandora was finishing a sale when the Goth girl came in. She handed her customer her package, thanking her, then looked over at the exotic creature thumbing through a rack of bras. "If you have any questions, let me know," Pandora said in Czech, not adding the part about the dressing room. She didn't look like she even wore underwear, let alone bathed. Pandora liked to think she didn't judge people by how they looked but she had to admit Mrs. Pinski had nabbed a couple of shoplifters. She walked over and stood beside the girl. "Find anything you like?" she asked cheerfully.

"I'm here about the job. The one in the paper?"

Pandora looked at her curiously. "Really. Well," she said, extending her hand, "I'm Pandora."

The girl shook it absently. "Lila," she mumbled, then sighed and looked around the room as if she weren't sure where she was. Pandora didn't know what to say. It hadn't occurred to her she'd need a script for the interviews.

"You don't seem to be much of a people person," Pandora ventured.

"People are scum," said Lila.

"You do know the job involves sales? I mean, hating people might not be a big plus."

This seemed to wake the girl up. "I knew you wouldn't like me," she said savagely, then tore a fistful of bras off the rack and shook it in Pandora's face. "This is bourgeois shit anyway." She threw it on the floor and stomped out.

That went well, thought Pandora as she picked up the merchandise. In the course of the next four days she had six interviewees, including a heavyset woman with a beehive hairdo and leopard tights who called her "sweetie," a young man whom she noticed sniffing a thong, a woman who smelled so strongly of garlic it made her eyes burn, and a woman who nearly made it out the door with an unpaid-for sixteen-hundred koruna negligée. Ty called moments after the latter was taken away by the police. "Maybe this was a mistake," said Pandora, shaken by the experience. "Maybe you're right, maybe I'm too much a control freak to let anyone else in here."

"Not wanting a stinker or a thief working for you doesn't make you a control freak," said Ty, as the doorbell dinged and a pretty dark-haired girl, her ballerina's body in a tight pink angora sweater, short black skirt, black tights and Doc Martin Mary Janes, entered the store. She stopped just inside, suddenly shy.

Pandora put the mouthpiece on her shoulder and addressed her in Czech. "Can I help you?"

"I'm, uh, here about the job?" the girl answered, her Czech slightly Slovak accented. "Is it still available?"

"Got to go, love you," Pandora quickly said into the phone and dropped it into its cradle. "Yes, the job is still available," she said, smiling, "let me get you an application." The girl approached the register counter warily.

"I'm Pandora," she said, giving her the form. "Here's a pen."

"Thank you," the girl said in English taking the paper and pen and beginning to fill it out on the counter. "I am Danka."

"You speak English."

"I study in school. It is perhaps not so good."

"It's fine. Better than my Czech."

"No, your Czech is good."

"You could tell I wasn't Czech."

"Well, perhaps a little," Danka said diplomatically.

"You are American?"

"Yes," said Pandora, "how could you tell?"

"By your teeth?" she said.

Pandora laughed, taken by surprise by her answer, and the girl smiled shyly.

"Do you have any retail experience?" Pandora asked hopefully. She had taken an instant liking to her.

"A little, part-time? At shop in Bratislava?" The floodgates opened. "But I am learning real fast and I am hard worker and I will do anything to work for you." Danka took a breath. "I mean, you have such beautiful things and you are so beautiful and I will be very good employee."

"Well, all right then," said Pandora as she returned to some work in the stockroom. Normally she wouldn't leave a stranger alone in the store but for some reason was totally comfortable with Danka. She was only back there a few minutes when the doorbell dinged. She stopped at the door when she heard Danka speaking to the customer in Czech. "Good morning. I love your hair. If you see anything you like I'll get Mrs. Pandora for you."

Smiling, Pandora returned to her stockroom work. A few minutes later she heard Danka's voice at the door.

"Mrs. Pandora? I am finish."

Pandora came out and accepted the application from Danka's anxious hand. As she took it to the register she spoke to the woman who had just entered, browsing through a rack of camisoles. "We just got those in. If you'd like to try anything, the dressing room is just through there."

Pandora sat down on the stool behind the counter and glanced over the application. "This looks very good. Of course, I'll need to check your references."

"You mean I have job?" Danka said breathlessly.

"Well, yes but don't you want to know the pay and hours?"

"I am sure they are good."

"OK, anyway, it's twenty hours a week, a hundred and fifty koruna an hour."

"Good," said Danka, nodding rapidly.

"All right, then, when can you start?"

"Now?" said Danka brightly.

"How about tomorrow morning at nine?" said Pandora, laughing at the girl's unbridled enthusiasm.

§

Pandora was sautéing onions and rice for risotto when Ty came into the kitchen taking off his jacket. "Who are you and what have you done with my wife?" he asked in mock horror.

"Keep it up, there's cold pizza in the fridge," said Pandora.

"I'm sorry, I'm sorry, I'm sorry," he said, kissing her on the neck.

"It's not like I never cook."

"It's been a while," he said, helping himself to a pinch of grated Reggiano.

"I've been a little busy." She turned around abruptly and put her arms around his neck. "But things are going to be better. A *lot* better."

"You found somebody."

"Not just somebody, I'd swear she fell from heaven."

"Did you check her references? I mean, that's great but you never know these days."

"I didn't just fall off the cabbage cart. Her previous employers, teachers, everybody, they love her."

"Sounds almost too good to be true."

"Just open the Champagne?" She nodded toward a bottle of "Veuve" chilling in ice.

"All right, then," said Ty, lifting the bottle dripping from the bucket and twisting off the cork, which exploded with a satisfying pop. "Now for my news," he said, pouring the wine into the waiting flutes. "How would you like to spend two weeks on Guadeloupe? It's a French island, supposed to be the best food in the Caribbean. Paradise. What do you say?"

"Yes. I say yes, yes, yes," the last part of this involving smothering him in kisses. "When?"

"It's a very exclusive resort. The first available date is the first week of August. OK?"

"Should be fine. It will give me a few months to train my new helper and be sure I can trust her alone. OK, I'm not a total Pollyanna."

§

Pandora crossed the street to the store the next morning at 8:30, and Danka was waiting by the door. "You're early, I said nine," Pandora said, juggling the bag with coffee and pastries as she searched for her keys in her purse.

"I can take that," said Danka.

"Right, thanks," Pandora said, giving her the bag. *Mrs. Pinski would have stood there looking at me*, she thought as she unlocked the door.

When they were in the store, she locked the door behind them and turned on the lights. Danka was awed that she had coffee and pastries for both of them. Then they got down to business as she ran through the basic operation for her protégé, writing up a sale, ringing up a sale, keeping the merchandise folded and neatly hung, clearing the dressing room of merchandise between customers and keeping the stockroom in order.

At 9:45 the UPS driver rapped on the door. "Everybody's early today," said Pandora as she went to let him in. Pandora smiled to herself when she saw his hand truck only had one box. It always struck her as odd that someone who hated carrying boxes would have chosen his line of work. "This is Danka, my new assistant," she told him in Czech, then, to Danka, "this is Jarda, the UPS god." She smiled again when Danka rushed to shake his hand.

"Very pleased to meet you," Danka said.

"Likewise," said Jarda, looking her over thoroughly enough to make her uncomfortable. She turned back to her straightening, allowing him the opportunity to memorize her ass.

"He's a pig," Pandora told Danka when he'd backed out of the store, "but it's always good to have the UPS driver on your side."

"Oh, I am used to this," said Danka, who wasn't used to it at all. Men's stares made her extremely uncomfortable; once she had literally run away, mortified, when a stranger began declaring his undying love for her at a bus stop.

"That's good, because the husbands buying gifts for their wives are worse. They'll be asking you to 'model' for them, just to be sure something fits." She opened one of the boxes. "Help me hang these things and I'll show you how to tag them and add them to the inventory list."

"Goodness," said Danka, lifting a lacy marvel from the box, "I am never seeing such beautiful things."

"A discount comes with the job. Try on anything you like."

"Anything?"

"Sure, half the fun of having a shop is playing dress up."

Danka showed her the merry widow Cerise bought. "Will this fit me?"

"I think it's too big," she said choosing another for her. "Take it in there and close the curtain, we need to open the store."

Danka disappeared into the dressing room as Pandora unlocked the door and flipped the sign from "*Zavřeno*" to "*Otevřeno*," then finished sorting out the cash register. Pandora looked up, thinking Danka was awfully quiet. "Are you OK in there?"

"Yes. Well, no, I'm afraid I don't know how this is working."

Pandora pulled the curtain aside. Danka had it on backwards. "Oh dear, let me help you," said Pandora stepping in. She unhooked it, and Danka turned to face her.

"God, your breasts are gorgeous," Pandora said, then shook her head. "I'm sorry, I can't believe I said that."

"But I'm afraid they are too small," said Danka.

"Don't be silly," said Pandora as she held the two sides of the corset together over Danka's breasts. "Here, hold it like this while I finish lacing the ribbon."

As Danka held the corset Pandora dropped to her knees and started lacing the ribbon that crisscrossed over the hook and eyelet fasteners.

"A Champagne coupe, the bowl-shaped glass that was supposedly modeled after Madame DuBarry's breasts, would fit perfectly over yours." Pandora recited a verse that had always cracked up her mother.

> *"Madame DuBarry was a lively old fairy*
> *Who sold herself to a king*
> *For diamonds and pearls*
> *While other poor girls*
> *Stayed pure and got nary a thing."*

Pandora looked up as she laced the ribbon. Danka, hypnotized by her touch, had her eyes closed.

"Did you understand any of that?"

"No. Well, some. It's poem, right?" murmured Danka.

"The point is she did just fine with her gorgeous small breasts."

"I still would rather have like yours."

Pandora stood up as she reached the top. "OK, bend over and lift like this," she said, demonstrating. Danka leaned over, slid her hands inside the corset and lifted her breasts so they exploded from above the Victorian garment as Pandora lace the rest of the ribbon, finishing with a lovely bow.

"There," said Pandora, turning her around to see herself in the mirror, her hands on the girl's bare shoulders. "Nothing wrong with those."

Danka's eyes widened as she looked at herself. "I can't believe this is me."

The doorbell signaled that a customer had entered, and Pandora gave her a pat. "Time to pay the rent," she said as she pushed passed the curtains.

"Mrs. Pandora?" said Danka, stopping her.

"Yes?"

"I am loving to be working under you."

"I love having you," said Pandora, marveling at how it had all worked out.

seven

And, indeed, Danka turned out to the exception to the too good to be true rule. She was doggedly efficient at restocking, inventory control, and bookwork, the nuts and bolts of running the store that had always bored Pandora, and she had a streetwise awareness that discouraged shoplifters as well as Mrs. Pinski had but without making the store feel like an internment camp. But most importantly, she could sell. When Pandora ran the numbers in her tiny home office, she ran them again to be sure there wasn't a mistake. There wasn't. The store had an astonishing

50% increase over the previous year. She showed the numbers to Ty.

"You've had increases every year since you opened," he said.

"Not like this."

Danka got a raise the next morning. Which was good, since she was spending most of their slow time trying things on, and even with the discount Pandora gave her, there wasn't going to be anything left come payday. That morning she was wearing a lavender silk camisole over tight jeans, the latter after Pandora insisted it was no problem for her to wear something to work that her boss wore nearly every day. Of course, she was braless, the camisole demanded it, and the UPS driver was apoplectic when she helped him with the day's delivery.

Pandora had worked till after midnight paying invoices and she gave Danka a stack of envelopes to mail at the post office, not wanting to wait for the postal carrier. As Danka was leaving Cerise entered. "Hi! Welcome to Pandora's Box," Danka said in Czech with a huge smile as she held the door for her, then practically skipped up the street.

"Who was that?" asked Cerise, in French as was now usual for them, kissing Pandora on both cheeks.

"My new employee."

"That's a dreadful dose of cheerfulness for so early in the morning."

"It's eleven."

"Well, I had a big night."

"She's been a lifesaver, literally," said Pandora.

"Your life seems fine to me," said Cerise, browsing the racks.

"My husband was ready to divorce me if I didn't start making time for him."

"*Cherie*, that husband isn't going anywhere. I see how he looks at you," she said, checking sizes on a waterfall of bras and panties. She held up a black lace bra. "Do you have another of these in my size in the back?"

"Everything I have is out, I'm afraid."

"Damn," said Cerise, putting the bra back.

"Don't you already have it?"

"Yes, I loved it. It was torn off me last night at work," she said, thumbing through another rack.

"Must have been quite a party," said Pandora, interested.

"Ooph," said Cerise, shaking her hand in the air and rolling her eyes for emphasis.

"So, spill. C'mon, what happened? Hurry, before Danka gets back."

"Ooph," she repeated, "I promise myself this every time, I'm only there to dance."

"You didn't just dance," said Pandora, now *very* interested.

"No." She picked up the same lavender camisole Danka had been wearing. "Isn't this what your new girl was wearing? It looked great on her but with my boobs—"

"Cerise, stop teasing me, what happened last night."

"OK," she said, hanging the camisole back on the rack. "I didn't just break my guideline last night, I smashed it into the ground."

"You had sex with one of the men?"

"Yes...and a few others."

"A *few*? What's a few?"

"At the same time, or in total?"

"Good heavens!" gasped Pandora, as the doorbell announced Danka's return.

"I'm Cerise," Cerise said in French, "Pandora has said such nice things about you."

"I'm sorry," said Danka in Czech, "I don't understand."

"*Ne parle pas francais?*"

"I am speaking English?" ventured Danka.

"*Désolé, je ne parle pas anglais.*"

"OK," said Danka, bewildered.

Knowing Cerise's game, Pandora interceded. "Why don't you unpack the box we got from Elfe today?" she said in Czech. "Perhaps there will be something Cerise will like."

"No problem," said Danka, and disappeared into the stockroom.

"You were saying?" said Pandora in French.

"Where was I? Oh, how many." She thought about it. "Well, there were nine men there, so I guess, totally, nine."

"My God," said Pandora. "And at the same time?" Cerise considered this problem. "Six. Definitely six." Pandora struggled to get her head around this. "Six? How is that even possible?"

"I guess it's a little like yoga," said Cerise as Danka came back and began to arrange the new stock on the respective shelves and racks. Cerise walked over to the rack with the camisoles and reconsidered the one Danka was wearing.

"That's incredible," said Pandora.

"Incredible doesn't begin to describe it, sweetie, these guys were gorgeous. It was some kind of football team but not, you know, real football."

"Were they Americans?"

"No, Austria? No, Australia, that's it."

"I can't even imagine it," wondered Pandora, as Danka returned to the stockroom for another load.

"Really? Haven't you ever wished just once in your life to be completely, I don't know, satiated? Completely and totally satisfied?"

"I thought I had been."

Danka returned with another armload of lacy confections, a little jealous to be left out of the conversation, and decided she would definitely have to learn French.

"Oh, that reminds me. I have a lunch date. Can you order that bra for me?"

"It's already on reorder. I'll save one for you."

"Will you have two in my size?"

"I think so."

"Save them both for me. My job is so hard on lingerie." She opened the door to leave. "Oh, you'd never guess who my lunch date is. One of the Australians!" Then she waved to Danka, "*Un plaisir de faire votre connaissance, Danka,*" and was gone in a breathless flurry.

"She seem very nice," said Danka.

"Cerise is a force of nature," said Pandora.

"What is nature force?"

Pandora tried to explain it in Czech.

"Oh, you mean she has a great lot of energy," said Danka.

§

Ty knew something was up as soon as he got home from work. For one thing, the house was dark, except for light coming from the bedroom at the top of the stairs. And he heard music up there as well, throbbing Electronica. "Panda?" he said, looking up from the bottom of the stairs. When he entered the bedroom she came out of the bathroom wearing a long tight black stretch-lace dress with nothing under it.

"I thought you'd never get here," she said, wrapping her arms around his neck and pressing her mouth to his. He kissed her back as long as he could, then pulled away.

"Aren't we going out to dinner tonight?" he wondered.

"I changed our reservation to later," she said, tearing at his clothes. "Do me a favor?"

"OK."

"Fuck me." She pushed him onto the bed, tore his pants and boxers off and threw herself on his cock, sucking it hard.

"OK," he said, more than a little bemused.

She lifted the dress to her waist and straddled him, rubbing her clit on his cock as she unbuttoned his shirt. Tearing it open, she fell forward, kissing his chest as she guided him into her now thoroughly wet pussy. Then she rolled them over so he was on top of her. "I mean it, fuck me, fuck me harder than you ever have."

Ty obliged, driving her two feet up the mattress, until she reached over her head, bracing herself on the headboard, her breasts heaving with each of his Herculean thrusts. His day had been unusually stressful and he'd canceled a handball game for their dinner date, so he had plenty to unwind, and he poured it all into his wife, bringing them both to a violent climax.

He rolled off her. "No going to sleep," she said, touching his nose.

"Don't worry, I'm starving." He got up on one elbow and looked at her, her face and chest still flushed with the excitement of the moment. "Not complaining, that was an amazing welcome home, but you were on fire. What got into you?"

"I don't know, I guess I've had a lot on my mind lately."

§

The next morning Danka opened the store by herself for the first time, allowing Pandora a few extra minutes to linger over breakfast and even enjoy coffee in her own kitchen. She had hoped to share it with Ty, but he had an early meeting. He was planning, however, to come by the shop to see her new window display and, not incidentally, meet Danka.

She took the opportunity to window shop on her way to work and didn't arrive till after ten. She felt positively liberated. Crossing the street, she was gratified to see several people gawking at her window. She was even more gratified when she entered the store to see Ty and Danka chatting amiably.

"You two seem to have hit it off."

"I think you scored," said Ty.

"I know I did," she said as she put her purse in the drawer under the register. "You're early. I thought you were taking me to lunch."

"Sorry, I got a meeting with another ministry that might help us."

"I know, with your permits. I'm sick of the permits."

"You didn't tell me Danka's a dancer," said Ty.

"Not anymore," said Danka, "now I am executive assistant."

"What's this about dancing?" asked Pandora.

"I came to Prague to study, with my friend. We were both at conservatory in Bratislava. She is very good. I am not so good, I'm afraid."

"Are you sure? I mean, if it's your dream."

Danka shook her head sadly. "Sometimes we need new dreams."

"Spoken like a philosopher," said Ty. He checked his watch. "Gotta run," he said, giving Pandora a peck on the cheek.

"He is very handsome and very nice," said Danka when he was gone.

"If I feel like smiling all I have to do is think about him," said Pandora as she went to the stockroom. Danka looked after her thoughtfully.

They had a flurry of lunchtime business that lasted till after one, so it was probably just as well Ty had his meeting, plus Pandora would have missed Cerise's big news. When she came in it was clear she'd been crying.

"Oh my God, Cerise, what's wrong?" Pandora asked, concerned.

"Nothing. Nothing's wrong in the whole world," Cerise announced, holding out her left hand and a huge yellow diamond.

"Wow, I've only seen a stone like that in magazines. Danka, look at this."

Danka thought Cerise was an idiot but she could see the special bond she had with Pandora, so was careful not to let it show. She oohed and awed politely over the ring. Cerise, for her part, wasn't fooled by her for a second but her way of dealing with it was to be extravagantly friendly and complimentary towards the girl. In other words, she wasn't an idiot, even if she played one for a living.

"It's fabulous. Who gave it to you?" Pandora said, moving her hand to catch the light.

"My Australian."

"Oh, Cerise, I'm so happy for you."

"I never thought it would happen."

"And I guess you don't have to worry about telling him—"

Pandora stopped herself, remembering Danka was there. "We got so busy we haven't had lunch," she said as Danka busied herself rehanging items that had been dumped in the dressing room. "Danka, take your lunch break now, and you can bring me back something."

"I brought a sandwich," said Danka.

"Then I think I'll hop out for a bite with Cerise."

They found an outdoor table at a nearby cafe and ordered Champagne to celebrate. "I started to say, I guess you won't have to worry about telling him about your job," said Pandora in French.

"You're right, there's no mystery about that. He had a front-row seat. He doesn't care. I mean, he doesn't want me to do it anymore, but he knows we all have pasts. Mine is just a little more interesting. I only have one more booking, a bachelor party for the fiancé of that von Aachental bitch, and I'm going to cancel it."

The waiter brought their Champagne and they toasted and sipped. Cerise was bubblier than the Champagne. "He gave it to me over cappuccinos. Do you think they have cappuccinos in Australia?"

Pandora was still thinking about Cerise's last dancing job. "You haven't canceled it?"

"Cancelled what?"

"The bachelor party."

"No, I need to call them. The poor boys will just have to watch a porn video and play with themselves."

"I want to do it." said Pandora abruptly.

"Watch porn and play with yourself?"

"No, take your place."

"Are you out of your mind?" said Cerise, wide-eyed.

"Maybe but I want to do it," said Pandora firmly.

"What have I done?" wondered Cerise.

"Created a Pandastein?" said Pandora.

"I appreciate you wanting to help me out but this isn't necessary."

"I'm happy if it helps you out but this is for me, something I need to do."

Cerise considered her friend gravely. "So be it." She waved to the waiter for another round, then leaned into her friend and lowered her voice, just in case someone at one of the other tables spoke French. "OK, the most important thing is to remember what you *aren't* there for. They're only paying you to dance, you don't have to fuck anybody."

"Like you always remembered."

"I never said I was perfect."

The bartender brought their Champagne, and Cerise waited till he'd gone back inside before she continued. "Wear something sexy but easy to take off, not too complicated, and be sure it's something you can live without. Sometimes boys break pretty things. Bring a CD that's easy to dance to, not too fast, about 88 beats per minute. Is this too technical?"

"No," laughed Pandora, sipping her wine. Cerise never failed to surprise her.

"But most of all, don't worry. You're so gorgeous you can just stand there and they'll be thanking whatever God they thank." She took a slip of paper from her purse. "Here's the address."

"What time?"

"Nine."

"Tonight," said Pandora, mostly because she wanted to hear Cerise say it, that it might all be real.

"Tonight."

Cerise reached into her shoulder bag and brought out a small purse, which she put on the table in front of Pandora.

"And take this."

"What is it?"

"Insurance," she said as she opened it and showed its contents to Pandora: a small camera, its lens fixed to a tiny hole in the side of the purse. "In case there is any trouble."

Pandora looks dubious.

"OK, maybe I am a bit of the voyeur. Now you know all my secrets."

§

Totaling the day's receipts, Pandora looked up as Danka got her purse from the drawer under the register. "We had a record day today. I need to place re-orders with four of our vendors."

"Great," said Danka, "have a good night," and she went out the door. Pandora followed her out stopping her before she crossed the street. "Danka, are you OK?"

"I'm fine."

"Is it Cerise?"

"It's stupid, I'm stupid, don't worry about it."

"You most certainly aren't stupid."

"I'm happy for her. Really."

Pandora saw an unsmiling girl directly across the street. "Who's that?"

"A friend," said Danka, seeming embarrassed.

"Is she your roommate?"

"Yeah."

"Tell her to come over, I'd like to meet her."

"I don't think she will."

"Why not?"

"She's weird. Anyway, I'll see you tomorrow," Danka said, crossing the street to the girl.

Pandora went back inside but looked at them through the window. They appeared to be arguing. Then she called Ty's office. When Mara answered she asked her if he was still there. When she heard his voice she had a moment of fear that she couldn't or shouldn't or wouldn't go through with her mad plan, while she heard her voice telling him there was something she had to do with Cerise that evening, "kind of a yoga thing," and she'd probably be late.

Pandora went by the house and chose an outfit, then returned to the little cafe where she'd met with Cerise, sitting inside this time, and ordered some grilled fish and a glass of white wine. But when the fish came she was too excited and anxious to eat.

As she sipped the wine she looked at the camera in the purse Cerise had given her. It was a half-frame camera, using 35mm film, a lover in Moscow had given her in the hopes she would provide him with compromising photos of a rival politician. It had a key wind and could be set to take a picture from every five seconds to one per hour. Cerise had it set on two a minute, which meant it would take seventy photos in a little over a half hour. She briefly considered leaving it behind, that she would have enough to worry about but she had to admit the thought of having pictures of her adventure was a turn on, especially since she didn't plan on becoming a regular on the exotic dance circuit. She wound up the camera and dropped it into her bag, along with a CD of Electronica music she'd made for the shop and a black Zorro mask Ty had worn for Halloween.

Pandora paid for her wine and uneaten fish, assuring the worried waiter that her tummy was just upset (which was true, only it wasn't a bug but butterflies that were bothering her) then returned to the shop to dress. For lingerie, she'd chosen a black lace set that included thigh high stockings, thong, and an extremely sheer lightly underwired bra that followed Pandora's curves exactly, and that did almost nothing to hide her nipples. For shoes, she had black patent pumps with four-inch heels, elegant and classic but more importantly, she knew she could dance in them without teetering like she was on a high wire.

Her dress was a simple black crepe sheath dress with a side zip (important!), low cut enough to show her cleavage to good advantage but quietly elegant.

Her black Armani trench coat added a note of mystery. She slid the CD and mask in her pocket, tucked Cerise's little bag under her arm and hailed a cab.

§

The party was at a condo in an upscale new building on the outskirts of the Smichov district, in other words, new money. During the relatively long cab ride, Pandora had time to worry for the first time that things didn't get *too* nuts. If she could have seen the scene she wouldn't have worried. The apartment was gorgeous, a modern concrete, stainless steel and glass aerie with a river view. Six very handsome men, ages roughly from thirty-five to forty-five, all but one in designer shirts and jeans, were seated on the white leather sofas and chairs surrounding vodka shots neatly lined up on a huge low glass table.

The guest of honor, Michal, soon to be married to the unpleasant countess, knocked down a shot and slammed the glass to the table, as 80's rock played on an elaborate B & O stereo system.

"OK," said Roman in Czech as he picked up a glass, "but I still say that it would be better to start now with a fiber optic network, rather than trying to piggyback DSL on our pre-war phone system." He downed his shot and carefully returned the glass to the table.

"Enough business, this is supposed to be a party," said Jan, the youngest of the group, picking up his shot. "Can we talk about something a little amusing?"

Bednar joined him, picking up a glass and toasting, "Yes, enough Silicone Valley, where's our valley of silicone?" They threw back the shots and slammed the glasses to the table.

"I agree," said Tesar, picking up a glass, "this is supposed to be a bachelor party, not a wake."

Hudak, the owner of the apartment, looked at his watch. "The silicone is due any minute."

"Please tell me you didn't get a stripper," said Michal.

"What is it with you?" scoffed Hudak. "You aren't even married yet and the countess already has you declawed. You know what comes next—"

"Neutering!" Michal's friends bellowed in unison.

Hudak refilled the glasses, laughing.

"Seriously," said Roman, undeterred, "do you know how much money could be made for building an entirely new network from the ground up?"

"Wouldn't fiber optics just be in the ground?" wondered Bednar.

"I am serious," Hudak said, glaring at Roman, "if you don't stop it we're going to toss you in the river. We could just about make it from here."

"All right," Roman said, picking up a glass and lifting it. "To the end of an era."

The rest lifted their glasses and crashed them into his, then dumped the sharp Russian liquor down their throats.

They were quiet for a moment, thinking about this, as Hudak refilled their glasses.

"So maybe it is a wake," said Jan. "Someone, anyone, rescue us, say something amusing."

"OK," said Roman, "what's the smallest bill you'd pick out of a public toilet?"

"What currency?" said Tesar, just as the apartment intercom buzzer sounded.

"The stripper!" shouted Jan as Hudak went to the door, "we're saved!"

"Easy for you to say," said Michal.

Hudak pressed the button and said hello, and they heard Pandora, speaking French, ask for Hudak. He buzzed her up. He turned to his expectant friends. "I think she was speaking French."

"It's OK, I know French," said Michal.

"Then there is no problem," said Hudak, opening the front door and looking into the hallway. A moment later the elevator doors opened and Pandora appeared, wearing the black mask. Hudak, self-conscious about his neighbors, frantically waved to her. She sauntered over, and he pulled her in, closing the door behind them, relieved no one saw.

"Are you Hudak?" said Pandora in French, taking off her coat.

Momentarily struck mute at their good fortune, Hudak just grinned at her.

"My coat?" said Pandora.

Hudak didn't understand French, but finally got what it meant when a stunning woman holds her coat out to you.

"Oh, sorry," he said in Czech, taking it.

"I must say I'm surprised to see you all," said Pandora, "I thought this was strictly a bachelorette party. Where's Beatrice?"

Suddenly alarmed, Michal jumped to feet and hurried over. "What's this about Beatrice?" he answered in French.

"Well, this is her party, isn't it?"

"No, it's mine. I'm Michal, her fiancé."

Pandora offered him her hand. "I'm Angelique, it's lovely to meet you."

"Her party is at the Bohemia," he said.

"I feel so foolish," said Pandora, "especially wearing this mask."

"I didn't know she was having a costume party," said Michal, wondering why she didn't take her mask off.

Pandora looked at the vodka bottle and shot glasses on the table. "As long as I'm here, might I have a drink?"

"What's going on?" said Tesar in Czech, "is she going to take her clothes off or not?"

"Cool it, she isn't the stripper, man, she's a friend of Bea's," he said testily. "And she doesn't know we're even having one."

"Is there a problem?" Pandora asked in French.

"No, please what would you like?" Michal replied.

"Champagne?" Pandora subtly sizing up the crowd as she looked around the room.

"Do you have any Champagne?" Michal asked Hudak in Czech.

"Are you kidding? That's all Maria drinks," he said as he went to the kitchen.

Pandora looked out the window. "My God, what a fabulous view."

Hudak came in with a bottle of Champagne and gave Pandora a flute. "*Merci*," she said, and he twisted off the cork with a satisfying pop and filled her glass. "*Merci beaucoup.*"

She turned and looked at the men, who were slack-jawed with awe. "So, what have you boys been up to?" she asked. Michal translated.

"Tell her we were talking about finding money in public toilets, chicks love that," said Roman in Czech.

"Is she going to take off her mask?" asked Tesar.

Cerise's purse under her arm, Pandora got the CD from her coat and went to the stereo. "OK if I put something else on?" she asked, not waiting for a reply, and a moment later throbbing Electronica bass and drums filled the apartment. She turned it up louder, then, her back to the men, released the timer on the camera and set the purse on the shelf beside the stereo so the lens took in the scene. She floated over to the men on the couch and started dancing.

"What are you doing?" said Michal, alarmed.

"Well, I think the reason you boys are so gloomy is you really were expecting a stripper, and she didn't show up. No?" She danced in front of Bednar, stroking his hair.

"Uh, Michal, is it OK if I enjoy this?" he said, worried about the countess.

Pandora unzipped her dress and lifted it over her head, stunning the men momentarily to silence. Then they cheered, except for Michal who vaulted from his chair, picked up her dress and tried to cover her. "My God, what are you doing?" he shouted.

"I thought you wanted a woman to take her clothes off for you."

"Yes, but not one of Bea's friends, for God's sake. She'll fucking kill me!" Michal said, the "she'll fucking kill me" in Czech not French, however.

Michal's friends were groaning now, drunk enough to be outraged that he was stopping the show.

"You've got to get out of here," Michal said, desperately.

"Michal?" said Pandora, calmly, draping her dress neatly over a chair, then resting her wrists on his shoulders. "I'm not one of your fiancée's friends. I don't even like her."

"You don't?" he said happily. That hadn't come out right. "I mean, you aren't?" he corrected himself.

"No, I'm the stripper."

He laughed. "You got me."

"So, it's OK?" said Tesar, in Czech.

"It's OK," said Michal, sitting down and beaming up at her. "*Mademoiselle, nous sommes vos esclaves*," he said, declaring them her slaves.

"No, I'm yours," said Pandora straddling him and running her fingers through his hair as she lap-danced and his friends cheered.

"Maybe I need to get married after all," said Roman, "so Huddie will throw me a party too."

It only took a moment of moving on Michal's lap, her breasts close to his face, for her to sense serious activity in his pants. She pressed her pussy against it, moving in rhythm to the music, his hands gripping the arm of the chair as his friends cheered. She moved his hands to her ass, then up to her breasts and his friends cheered louder.

"Jesus, is she supposed to do that?" wondered Tesar.

"Who cares, I just want to know if we get a turn," said Bednar.

As if in answer to Bednar's question (which he assumed she couldn't understand), and not wanting Michal to come in his pants, Pandora kissed him, ruffled his hair and stood up, teetering in her pumps after all due to a slight erotic weakness in the knees.

She moved catlike among the men. Circling behind them, she pressed her breasts against Hudak's head as she ran her hands down his chest, then twisted Roman's face around and buried his nose in her cleavage as she climbed over the back of the sofa and straddled him, holding his head against her breasts as she moved on him until she felt the hardness in his jeans rubbing against her pussy. When she was sure he was rock hard, and in spite of his disappointed protestations, she slipped over onto Hudak's lap, letting him bite at her nipples through the transparent lace of her bra as she rocked her hips, feeling his cock growing in his pants until she was sure she could make out the tip through the thin wool of his suit pants.

Now it was Bednar's turn. She crawled across the low table and into his lap, braced herself against the back of his leather chair and undulated on his already hard cock while the men hooted and crowed. Before he could come in his pants, she moved on to Tesar, cradling his head in her breasts as she pushed her pussy against his cock in time with the pounding bass and drums. She looked around at the men, now unselfconsciously rubbing their cocks through their pants as she danced on the lucky man.

"Have I missed anyone?" she said in French, clearly framing it as a question.

Jan's entire French vocabulary consisted of oui and merci but he got it instantly. "Me!" he said in Czech, raising his hand like a schoolboy, and Pandora climbed off Tesar and danced slowly over to him, alone in an oversized white leather chair. She bent over in front of him letting him admire her cleavage while arching her back so the rest could noisily enjoy the twin globes of her ass. Jan reached for her in frustration, but she pushed his hands away and circled him, running her fingers through his hair and down his chest, then straddled him and danced with abandon, her mind racing with the thought of the hard cocks straining against their jeans in her honor. Jan came in his pants, creating a more-than-respectable wet spot.

"Oh dear," she said in French, adding, "It's OK, it's natural, no?" His friends weren't so kind, jeering at him in Czech.

"I couldn't help it," he protested.

Pandora looked at Michal, who was laughing to tears. "All right, hotshot, let's see how long you can last," she said, straddling him again. She kissed him, moving her pussy on his aching cock, then, very slowly and ceremoniously unhooked her bra, and the men quieted, shocked.

She hung her head back, her hair on her shoulders, and Michal kissed and sucked her breasts. Then she slid off him onto her knees, running her hands up and down his thighs in time to the music, each time closer to his cock, until he felt her hand pressing on it. Feeling it throbbing under his jeans, she leaned in and kissed it, then turned her head and gently bit it through the denim, causing the wide-eyed Michal to gasp as he gripped the arms of the chair. The men watched, awed, as she unbuttoned his jeans and slid them from his hips and off his legs, his aching cock tenting the thin fabric of his boxers. These too (the boxers) were quickly disposed of and Pandora found herself face-to-face with a very hard, very impressive cock. She seized it in her fist, and another shudder ran through Michal's body. She looked up into his eyes. "Please, sir, would you like to fuck my mouth?" she said softly.

"*Oui, s'il vous plait*," he said, choking out the words.

"No problem," she answered, his head spinning, and she teased the tip with her tongue, then took it in her mouth, tonguing it as she stroked the shaft. No longer able to resist, Michal took her head in his hands, oblivious to the room, his friends, his future wife or what year it was, as he pushed his fingers into her hair and her head down on his throbbing cock. Feeling it at the back of her throat, Pandora rose up slightly higher to get a better angle, then took the entire shaft into her mouth, the tip pushing into her pharynx and her lips at the base.

"Oh, my God," whispered Bednar in Czech, "I saw this in a video once but I figured they did it with special effects."

Pandora rose up, gasping for breath, then, applying gentle suction, her head bobbing in his lap, brought Michal to screaming climax, his cock pumping an impressive amount of cum into her mouth with each throb.

Sensing his sudden sensitivity, she stopped but kept his shaft in her mouth as she swallowed his cum. Then she looked up and smiled, wiping her lips lightly.

"*Est-ce OK?*" she smiled.

"*C'était fantastique,*" he gasped, catching his breath.

Pandora pushed herself to her feet, lightheaded herself. The men looked up at her, afraid to breathe, completely at sea. She started with Hudak. Kneeling before him she undid his belt, then unbuttoned his suit pants and slid them to the floor. He was wearing stupid bikini brief underwear (surprise!), his cock protruding from under the band. "*Ooh la la,*" said Pandora, finding them more than slightly ridiculous, and pulled them down around his ankles before they could spoil the vibe. She seized his cock in her fist, stroking it as she smiled up at him, her mouth close enough to it, he could feel her breath.

"*Být,*" he pleaded, and she happily complied, taking it her mouth as she watched his eyes. But when it was as hard as it could be, she stood before him and eased off her thong, then took his hand as she lay back on the low table.

"*Baise-moi, být,*" she said, as she guided him down on top of her, and he entered her smoothly, her wetness inspired by all that cocksucking. At that moment the song changed on Pandora's CD to a slower, moodier piece, throbbing with bass guitar, and he thrust into her in time, crushing his chest on her breasts. Beginning her climb to climax, Pandora gasped with each thrust as he pushed deeper into her, her nails striping his back deep enough to draw blood, until he stiffened and cried out shooting his cum into her.

"Fuck, I can't believe this," said Roman quietly from the other couch.

"I believe it," said Jan. "I do."

Hudak rolled off of her, staggering back to the sofa and Pandora rose like Venus from the half shell and circled the room, a siren, hooking her finger first at Tesar, then Bednar, then Roman and finally Jan, beckoning them to their feet. She pulled them close to her kissing them as she tore at their clothes, until, with their help, she was surrounded by four naked men but more importantly, by four very hard cocks.

She pushed Tesar onto the table onto his back and started sliding her clit on his cock, her astonishing ass in the air before Bednar's unbelieving eyes. She looked back at him, what are you waiting for? He knelt behind her and entered her pussy, fucking her doggy style. But she pulled away, reaching back and guiding his cock, slick with a combination of her wetness and Hudak's cum, into her butt cleavage. Then Tesar's monster cock replaced Bednar's in her pussy, her full weight pushing it deep inside her.

"*Baise mon bouche!*" she cried hoarsely to Roman, reaching out and guiding his cock into her mouth.

Stroking it she looked to Jan. "*Tu aussi*," she said taking his cock in her fist and sucking it. Now she took them both in her mouth, rolling her hips on Tesar's cock as Bednar's slid in the deep cleavage of her ass. Then Bednar placed the wet tip against her pink bud, teasing it and she froze for a moment, concentrating on relaxing as he pushed it into her, inching his way deeper, until he was fully inside her and she began to move again against the four cocks throbbing in her mouth and pussy and ass, whimpering and crying and finally wailing as she climaxed so hard everything momentarily went black.

Fortunately, she was well supported by the four men. First Roman and Jan screamed as they shot twin jets of cum into her mouth, followed by Bednar and Tesar, their bodies convulsing as they pumped their cum into her pussy and ass.

All five were quiet for a moment, frozen in time. Then they realized where they were and what had just happened. Bednar gently pulled his cock from her and sat back and Jan and Roman lowered her to the table, rolling her off Tesla, his arm over his eyes as he caught his breath.

"Are you OK?" said Michal, worried.

She opened her eyes and smiled. "Better than OK." She sat up, and looked around her, dazed and a little confused. The men just watched her, awed and unsure. She leaned over and picked up her bra and panties, then looked up at Michal.

"Would it be OK if I took a quick shower?"

Michal translated for Hudak, who said, "Of course," in Czech and guided her to the bath. "Please, through here."

She picked up her shoes and dress, and, of course, Cerise's purse from the stereo and followed him to the bathroom, pausing to ask Michal to call her a cab. She closed the door of the granite, glass, and steel bathroom, carefully laying out her clothes beside one of the sinks and took off the mask. The woman in the mirror was disheveled but glowed with sex.

When she came back, freshened up, dressed and her makeup (beneath the mask) repaired, the men were dressed as well. They shuffled awkwardly, and she thought it was so funny that they were embarrassed, she kissed each one of them, leaving bright red lips on their cheeks they'd need to wipe off before they saw their wives, girlfriends and, in Michal's case, fiancée from hell. The cab buzzed, Hudak gave her a fat envelope, and Michal brought her coat.

At the door, she touched his cheek. "You're a sweet man, she's luckier than she knows," she said, and he watched her walk to the elevator, the poetry of her ass etched indelibly in his memory.

As the doors hissed shut she leaned in the corner watching the numbers tick by, then saw her reflection in the polished stainless steel and remembered the mask. She left it hanging from the handrail.

§

Once safely ensconced in the back seat of the cab, she looked up at the light in the window, high above them as the driver pulled away from the curb. She had no idea how long it had been since she'd walked into that building. She opened the purse and looked at the number in the little window on the back of the camera. All seventy shots had been fired. She put her head back on the seat and watched the city float by as if in a dream.

Pandora let herself in quietly and looked upstairs. The bedroom was dark. She slipped off her pumps, switched off the hall light and climbed the stairs in semi-darkness. After stowing Cerise's purse in her office desk drawer, she tiptoed into the bedroom, quietly unzipped her dress and hung it in the closet. Then she took off her bra and panties and slipped into bed. Ty stirred, "Hmm...sleepy."

"I know," she whispered as she snuggled in behind him, kissing him between the shoulder blades as they made the spoons.

§

Ty was up and gone early, careful not to wake her. She padded around the townhouse still a bit dazed, enjoying her coffee in her thick fluffy cotton robe in the window box with the river view, her knees up to her chest. When she got to the shop, things were already humming, with a customer in the dressing room and Danka helping another. When Cerise came in just after noon, they'd already had five sales. She took Pandora's arm, conspiratorially, speaking in French.

"The agency just called, they got three new bookings for me this morning. What happened last night?"

This wasn't a conversation to have in the shop with Danka and two customers. Pandora opened the drawer under the cash register and removed Cerise's camera purse. "Let's get some coffee."

They went to the same cafe. Regarding them as practically regulars now, the waiter asked if they wanted Champagne. Pandora, who usually didn't drink during the day, especially a school day, said no, just coffee.

"The same," said Cerise.

"American?" he asked because of Pandora's accent, meaning the kind of coffee she wanted.

"No, coffee," said Pandora, smiling, and he brought them demitasses of thick black espresso, along with fresh cream and a crystal sugar bowl.

"So, spill," said Cerise, in French so she wouldn't be slowed down mentally translating their conversation into English.

"Well, for the life of me I can't figure out how you managed six at once."

"*Oh...mon...Dieu*, you didn't?"

"I tried my best. Four was the most I could comfortably manage. Although one of them wasn't really all that comfortable. One of those pleasure vs. pain things?"

Cerise bit her lip. Pandora laughed. "Don't worry, they were very nice."

"How many were there?"

"Six."

"And you, you know, with four of them?"

"No, all six but only four at once."

"Only," said Cerise. She sipped her coffee. "I'm almost afraid to ask if now you want these new bookings."

"No thanks. It was a fun place to visit but I wouldn't want to live there. In other words, I'm not planning on quitting my day job, to say nothing of my marriage."

"I'm happy to hear this," said Cerise, genuinely relieved.

"Oh, here's your camera," said Pandora, giving her the purse.

"Did you use it?" she said.

"Yes, but I think I'll need to find a special place to develop these particular photographs."

Cerise took a pen a paper from her bag. "Here's the lab I've used. They are very discreet," she said, writing down the name and address. "And speaking of discreet...I don't know how to say this...have you had sex with Ty since?"

"No, he was asleep when I got home and left before I was up."

Cerise wrote another name on the paper. "Here's my doctor. I know how important he is to you."

"Like I said, they were very nice boys."

"Panda, you haven't been single in a long time." She pushed the paper across the table. "Be sure you aren't bringing home anything."

"I have a gynecologist."

"Just this once you might want to see someone else."

"You're right," said Pandora, slipping the paper into her bag. Cerise started to put the camera purse in her bag but noticed there was something in it besides the camera. She opened it and took out the envelope Hudak had given Pandora as she was leaving.

"What's this?" she said.

"I thought you should have it, since it was your job."

"No, you earned it," said Cerise pushing it back to her.

"God, I hope not," said Pandora. "I'd rather think of myself as a tourist, or hobbyist?" she laughed. "Anyway, please keep it. I worry about you. I mean, I know you have your Australian and everything—"

"Oh, that isn't all I have. OK, I have a confession to make. When I said I spent every extra penny in your shop it was only half true. I've saved half of everything I've made since I started dancing. My plan is to start a shop of my own, an aerobics studio but a special kind of aerobics. I want to teach women how to dance the way I dance, so their husbands want to stay home at night. Only now it will be in Sydney."

"It's a wonderful idea," Pandora said, pushing the money back across the table. "So add this to the kitty. This way you'll be one step closer to your dream, and I won't lose my amateur status."

Cerise shrugged and put the envelope into her bag, laughing, "So you will still be qualified for the Olympics."

§

Pandora left the undeveloped film canister at the bottom of her shoulder bag with her lipsticks and mascara, keys, receipts, birth control pills and Kleenex travel pack but she took Cerise's advice about the doctor. In fact, she got an appointment with her that afternoon, although the test results would take several days. That night Ty came home with another surprise; he'd instructed his attorney to make the minister an offer on the villa. She jumped him, wrapping her arms around his neck and her legs around his waist and smothered him with kisses.

"Let me know how you really feel about it," he laughed.

That night when she slid into bed Ty's cock was reliably already hard, but Cerise's caution was still on Pandora's mind. She said, "Come in my mouth? I've been thinking about it all day." Which was not only convenient but true. She piled pillows against the headboard, sat up, and pulled him onto her, pressing his cock between her breasts, and he fucked them. Fucking her tits was one of his favorites, and it wasn't long before he was making the tiny whispering groaning noises she recognized as a prelude to shooting a huge load of cum onto her neck and face. But, much as she loved feeling his hot cream on her cheeks and eyes, tonight she wanted her drink; she placed her hands on his hips to stop his thrusts and put the tip of her tongue under the tip of his cock and he held his breath as she teased it until he could take it no more and pressed his fingers through her hair, gripped her head firmly in his hands and thrust it hard between her lips, saying, "Jesus, Panda."

She looked up into his eyes, sucking, the tip fitting perfectly in the roof of her mouth. Watching his face. Watching his face. Moaning, he thrust hard, fucking her mouth hard, feeling the tip push against her throat. Holding his hips firmly, she pushed him away, then back again, guiding his thrusts until she'd taken in the entirety of it, until he plunged every inch deep into her throat, her nose against his belly. Still holding his hips, she pushed him out, gasped for breath then pulled it back in as far as it would reach, then started scratching his balls, and he screamed, his cock throbbing and his body shuddering with the force of each powerful ejaculate. Before that night, the most Pandora had counted was four. Tonight, she got five.

§

For days after "the big night" Pandora felt she was still walking in a dream, although reality intruded enough to keep her on planet Earth. The minister turned down Ty's offer, countering with one that was ridiculously more than they could afford. On the plus side, she found a great bikini for their Caribbean trip, and Cerise's doctor called her and said the tests were all negative. She hung up the phone, making a mental note that she would fuck Ty's brains out after three days of sucking his cock, which for her was the ultimate foreplay.

eight

Danka finished ringing up a customer, bagged her purchase in tissue and thanked her. As the woman left, Danka looked at Pandora, her hand still on the phone, thoughtful.

"Everything OK?"

"Fine," said Pandora, snapping out of it.

"You've been funny all week."

"I know. I have a lot going on. We made an offer on a house we really wanted but it wasn't good enough."

"I thought it might have something to do with Cerise."

Pandora had noted never to underestimate Danka. "It appears she'll be moving to Australia."

"Friendship is funny, isn't it?" said Danka as she went to check the dressing room.

"It is," said Pandora. "Thanks for opening again today, you've been a lifesaver."

"I like being this lifesaver," she said, returning the tried-on items to their racks and shelves.

Pandora looked at the clean counter. "Anything I need to deal with?"

"We have wonderful new things from La Mer. Would you like me to be model?"

One of Pandora's favorite things about having Danka there was playing dress-up when they didn't have a customer. "I would love that."

"I'm sorry my roommate was not polite the other day," said Danka as she took a sheer push-up bra to the dressing room.

"I figured she was just shy. How long have you been roomies?"

"Two years, counting at school."

"That's a long time."

"I know, maybe too long. Come see me?"

"Sure," said Pandora. She pulled the dressing room curtains aside. The bra looked wonderful on the girl, who had taken her jeans off as well for full effect.

"Are you liking me in this?" asked Danka, arching her back for full effect as she looked at herself in the mirror.

Before Pandora could answer, the doorbell dinged. As she looked out, two men wearing shabby ill-fitting suits entered, the first instructing the second in Czech to lock the door.

"Can I help you?" said Pandora, in Czech.

"Check the back," the man instructed his partner, ignoring her.

"What's going on?" said Pandora, getting angry.

"You are Mrs. Krizova?" the man asked in English.

"Yes," Pandora answered, glaring. "What's the meaning of this?"

"I think you are knowing what is the meaning of this," he said.

The other guy said "Look what I found" in Czech as he led the cowering Danka, still wearing nothing but the completely sheer bra and panties, out of the dressing room and marched her to the front of the store.

"Take your hands off her, she had nothing to do with it!" shouted a very agitated Pandora. "This is ridiculous! It was a very, very private party and this is supposed to be a free country?"

"I know nothing about any parties," said the English-speaking one. "You are to leave these premise immediately. They are confiscate."

"This isn't about the party?"

"This is about gangster husband. All your assets are seized," he said.

"May I get dressed first?" said Danka in Czech.

"You are Slovak," the second guy said.

"Yes," said Danka, covering her breasts.

The second guy looked at the first, who shook his head. "I don't like what is going on here with young naked Slovak girls." He sneered at Pandora, not bothering with English, "We are sick of you foreigners stinking up Prague with your money and pervert." He looked at Danka, "Put on clothes, you come with us."

§

To add insult to injury, there were two uniformed cops outside the door of the townhouse, one of whom stopped Pandora when she tried to go in.

"I live here," she protested in Czech.

"No one may enter," the cop said.

"Can I at least get my toothbrush and some clothes?" she asked, trying her best to control herself and appeal to whatever chivalry was left behind the badge.

The cop looked at his partner, who shrugged. "Go ahead," he said. "But make it snappy."

Pandora ran up the stairs to the bathroom and put a toilet kit together, then threw it in a suitcase, along with blouses, a skirt, jeans, shoes and underwear. The phone by the bed rang. She looked down the stairs. The cops were leaving her alone so far. She picked up the phone and heard Ty's voice. "Panda! Are you OK?"

"They seized the shop. My God, what is happening?" she whispered.

"I've been arrested."

"Why?"

"I'm not sure of the real reason but they're throwing the book at me. They just added white slavery of Slovak girls, for God's sake."

"They took Danka away."

"Well, that explains that part."

"How can this be, you've been scrupulously careful since we've been here, haven't you?"

"Absolutely. I think it has something to do with our 'friend,' the minister. He seems to have done a very efficient job of setting me up."

"I told you to let him win those tennis matches."

"I did."

"Are they going to deport us?"

"It may go worse than that," he said.

"How could it be worse than losing everything and being deported?"

"I may be taking that vacation by myself."

"My God, Ty, you mean—" Pandora heard muffled voices. Abruptly he came back on the line, "I gotta go. My lawyer has a room for you at the Hotel Palace. I'll call you there. Love you." Before she could answer he was gone. She hung up the phone. The first cop was standing in the door.

§

Pandora checked into the hotel, rich with old-school elegance. They had stayed here on their first nights in Prague; it had been a kind of second honeymoon. She went to the window, which looked down on Wenceslas Square, where hundreds of thousands of people had jangled their keys in defiance and brought down the communist government. Often when he would come up against a wall of intransigent bureaucracy or backward-thinking technocrat Ty would calmly explain that a half century of political trauma, first courtesy of the Germans, then the Russians, gave the Czechs the right to be grumpy about foreigners but that held little comfort for her now, with her husband in prison and all they'd worked so hard for seemingly snatched away.

She opened her suitcase. She'd barely had time to grab some underwear, a pair of jeans, a couple of tops and sneakers, besides a few toiletry items. Ty's hearing was scheduled for the next day; she'd have to wear what she'd worn to work. But that was nothing compared to what Ty faced. He didn't know how his attorney could prepare for the case in such a short time.

Pandora hated the thought of going out alone, so ordered room service, the TV droning in an unsuccessful attempt to stop her racing mind. She took a sleeping pill with the last of the Champagne from the split she'd ordered with her dinner but thrashed about wide awake for most of the night anyway. When she finally slept, she dreamt they were back in Santa Barbara, the dream so vivid she could feel the sun on her face and smell the ocean as they walked on the beach. She woke and groggily reached out for him, desperately unhappy when her hand only found an empty pillow beside her.

She had breakfast in her cafe near the shop. Everything seemed completely normal. The waiter waited, the customers ate. The people passing in the street the same as they had been on all those days she'd taken their lives for granted. Afterwards, she walked out into the sunshine, unsure of whether she should go by the shop, unsure of what she would find and how she would deal with it. Of course, she couldn't resist seeing it.

There was an official sign on the door warning anyone who might be thinking about entering to forget about it. Which meant her customers would know she'd run afoul of the law. The window displays were gone. She pressed her face against the glass, shielding it from the glare of the sun, and saw the racks and shelves had been stripped. Police girlfriends, and maybe even a few of their wives, were undoubtedly enjoying beautiful new underthings.

§

Pandora arrived at the courthouse early. She'd bought a coffee but dropped it in the trash, deciding she was wired enough. Vasek, Ty's lawyer, arrived and hugged her.

"I'm sorry about this," he said in English, "Ty doesn't deserve it. But this sort of thing goes on every day here."

"Is he going to be OK?" she said, searching his face.

"I don't know. All their evidence is from this Demkakova, but the guy's a bloody minister and *very* close to the president. It's all fabricated but even though Ty is Czech, he's still an outsider in their eyes, so anything we say is immediately discounted."

A guard opened the doors to the courtroom and Vasek put his hand on her back and guided her in. "It could be worse. They own the police," he said quietly. "They could have dug up anything they wanted from the evidence room to stick on him."

He pointed out a chair for her in the gallery immediately behind the defendant's table, and she sat behind him, fidgeting until Ty was brought in. When he hugged her over the railing she started to cry.

"It's going to be alright," he assured her, wiping her tears.

"I'm just so frightened."

"We'll get through this," he said, kissing her. As they sat down, several other people took seats in the gallery. Pandora wondered if they were witnesses, press, or just someone curious about this American criminal. Then Hudak walked through the door, she'd swear wearing the same suit as he'd had on at the bachelor party. He hadn't seen her without the mask but just to be safe she turned her head quickly before he saw her.

She leaned on the rail and whispered to Ty, "What's he doing here?"

"Who?" he said without looking up from some notes Vasek had him reviewing.

"Him," said Pandora, jerking her head toward Hudak.

"That's Demkakova, the fucking minister."

"No kidding," said Pandora, standing along with everyone in the room as the judge entered.

She kissed Ty and walked out with Vasek when it was over, checking the hallway before entering it to be sure Hudak was gone. She hadn't turned her head again after Ty told her who Hudak was, and he'd left without being called. Yes, there was the mask, and he was really drunk by the time she'd arrived, but she was still processing this amazing revelation. Hudak wasn't called because the judge had granted Vasek's request for more time to present a defense.

"Our attorney is a genius," she said, hugging Vasek.

"My brilliance had nothing to do with it," he said, "Demkakova owns that judge. By granting us a continuance he was buying insurance in case anyone questions his impartiality."

"Well, it isn't over yet."

"I don't know, Pandora. I wish I could say that but we're playing with their rules, their ball and their pitch," he said, revealing his British-taught English.

"It isn't over yet," she repeated firmly.

§

As she walked away, she thrust her hand into her shoulder bag, searching with her fingers until she found the film canister and gripped it in her fist. Then she saw Hudak, smoking a cigarette and talking to an older, well-dressed gentleman. He turned his head as she passed but her glance confirmed he was more interested in her tits than her face. She was sure he didn't recognize her.

§

The film lab was in an alley in Old Town, probably pre-war, including the grimy windows and peeling paint on the door. The place was so tiny, Pandora found it hard to believe they did as much business as Cerise had said. But, in fact, the actual lab was in Slovakia, which meant it definitely wasn't a one-hour photo. The kid behind the counter looked like he was twelve. Well, fourteen, considering his astonishing crop of acne. It occurred to Pandora this was a teenage dream job: processing the work of most of the erotic photographers and filmmakers in Prague. Pandora put the 35mm film canister on the counter.

"I'd like three eight-by-tens of each," she said in Czech.

The kid grunted as he wrote this down.

"How soon can I have them?"

The kid scratched his face as he thought about this, and she tried to look anywhere but his cheek, which was bleeding slightly.

"Least a week."

"Any chance I can get them sooner than that? They're very important."

He looked her over and was suddenly as interested as she was in seeing them as soon as possible. "Three days but it'll cost extra."

"No problem," she said. He noted it and offered her the claim check, which she took gingerly, trying not to think about where his fingers had been.

Back in the hotel room, the first thing she did was try Danka's number again but there was still no answer. She'd asked Vasek to check on her, making it clear it was important. She looked out the window onto the square, teeming with tourists filling their day with the living museum that was Prague. She needed to get out of her room. She was jumping out of her skin with anxiety but she wanted to be near the phone in case Ty called. Then it rang, and she ran to it.

"Ty?"

"It's me," said Cerise. Pandora had left a message on her machine the day the police had shown up. She had begun to worry about her too. "I'm sorry I do not call you. I go to Italy with Malcolm. They are in the finals now. Are you OK?"

"It's been a hellish week."

"Have you closed the shop?" asked Cerise.

"It wasn't my idea. Ty is having trouble with the government. He's been arrested."

"*Mon Dieu.*"

"I'd rather not talk on the phone. Do you have time for lunch?"

§

They met in their cafe, and seeing the two beautiful women again obviously made the waiter's day. She'd come to really feel that Prague was home but since Ty's arrest she'd never felt lonelier. Seeing Cerise was a huge relief, her news not so much.

"Malcolm's team will fly home this week and he wants to take me with him."

"That's wonderful, Cerise," Pandora said, putting her hand on her friend's. "I couldn't be happier for you."

"But I feel bad leaving you now. What will you do if Ty—" She stopped herself.

"If he goes to prison? I'm not going to let that happen." Said Pandora firmly.

"What can you do? They have the police and the judges and the government."

"I think I have something that will trump them all," said Pandora, switching to French. "You know the pictures I took with your secret camera? Guess whose bouncing lily-white ass is in them—the fucking minister who's trying to destroy us."

"*Mon Dieu*," said Cerise, for the second time that day. "But these people can be very dangerous."

"I'm not afraid of the guy after seeing him naked in a big chair drunkenly masturbating," Pandora said, wishing she knew how to say "jerking off" in French.

"I'm serious," said Cerise, obviously worried. "Many of these people were secret police before the revolution came and they changed their colors overnight."

"I understand," said Pandora, "I hate the thought of you living on the other side of the world but it's probably good you won't be in Prague when—" She tried to think about how to say "when the shit hits the fan" in French but settled for "when this breaks."

"It's true," worried Cerise, "it would only take a call to my agency for them to find me."

"But there is something you could do, something that would help Ty and protect me."

"Anything," said Cerise.

"When is your flight?"

"Friday."

"The prints will be ready. Take copies with you. If anything happens to me, send them to <u>Právo</u>."

Pandora was confident the left-wing newspaper would be all over the story.

"This is like a spy novel."

"I wish that's all it were," said Pandora.

They ordered more Champagne and talked about Cerise's erotic aerobics school and the babies Malcolm wanted and the amazing unpredictability of life, until they hugged each other tearfully and Pandora returned to her empty hotel room to wait.

§

The next three days were the longest of Pandora's life, the only high points when Ty was able to call her, even though the prison phone made it sound like he was in Siberia. There was still no answer on Danka's phone, and for the first time, Pandora started to worry about money. The prints had been promised for Thursday but when she called, the pimple kid told her they hadn't been in that morning's shipment, which usually arrived between eight and ten in the morning. He told her to check back the next day. Cerise's flight was at three in the afternoon. Pandora could put one set of prints in a safe deposit box they kept at a bank they only used for that purpose, which was why they weren't completely broke but the only people she trusted to deal with them if something bad happened were Danka and Mrs. Pinsky. She still didn't know where Danka was and was pretty sure Mrs. Pinsky would have a heart attack if she opened the envelope before giving it to the newspaper.

On Friday morning she didn't bother to call but went straight to the film lab storefront at nine. The prints were there. She had a feeling they'd been "quality checked" by everyone who worked there, because the kid was stupid nervous with her, and two men from the back she hadn't seen on her first visit came out to "do some filing," which included giving her a copious amount of surreptitious attention. It was nice to see people who enjoyed their work as much as these three.

§

Pandora left one set of the photos in their safe deposit, self-consciously separating them from their other duplicates as the bank clerk waited. She had thought about just showing up at Demkakova's office but it was Friday and she was afraid he'd already be gone, so she called his office for an appointment, speaking in her very best Czech. The receptionist, a woman with a very young-sounding voice, was instantly dismissive, telling her she couldn't possibly see the minister that afternoon. In fact, he didn't have an opening in his calendar for at least two months.

"Tell him my name is Angelique."

"I can't interrupt his meeting."

"Tell him Angelique needs to see him this afternoon. It's very important. If you don't, I promise you'll be just another secretary looking for work on Monday."

"I'm not a secretary," the girl sniffed, "I'm an executive assistant. Hold please." Two minutes later she was back. "The minister will see you at two p.m.," she said, clearly surprised.

"Tell him I'll be there at four," said Pandora, who wanted to see the second set of prints safely off to Australia before she walked into the lion's den.

Pandora took a cab to the airport, jammed with the summer's first crop of tourists, and pushed through the throng to the Qantas desk. Cerise and her fiancé had just checked in and were walking toward security, Cerise anxiously scanning the crowd for her. Tearful hugs were exchanged, along with a quiet transfer of a manila envelope from Pandora's shoulder bag to Cerise's. Introductions were made, Pandora noting both how impossibly handsome and viral Malcolm looked, and that he shook her hand instead of hugging her on their introduction, *and* he looked her in the eye and not at her chest when he spoke to her. The boy was in love.

§

Pandora walked into the minister's office exactly at four. Hudak's "executive assistant" was indeed young, and very attractive. Pandora was pretty sure she'd seen her in the shop. Hot lingerie could probably qualify as a business expense for an ambitious, career-minded young woman in Prague. She buzzed her boss, announcing "Angelique," and his voice came on the box instructing her to send the visitor in.

§

Demkakova's office in the lovely old building was polished hardwood and leather, as beautiful as it had been on the nineteenth-century day it was built, one of the advantages the Czechs enjoyed by not having put up too much of a fuss with either the Germans or Russians. Hudak stood as she entered, looking at her curiously.

"You were at the hearing," he said in Czech. "Angelique, isn't it?" He indicated a chair in front of his desk. "Please, have a seat."

Pandora sat, folding her hands over the manila envelope in her lap as he sat back down behind his desk. "So," he said, "I seem to be seeing quite a lot of you lately."

"And I you," said Pandora in English. "But my name is actually Pandora Krizova."

"*Mrs. Tybor* Krizova, I presume?" he said, his British-inflected English excellent.

"That's correct."

"Well, if you're here about his case, there's nothing I can do."

"I think there is."

"You may think whatever you like," he said, opening a cigarette box. He started to take one, then remembered his manners and offered it to her.

"No thank you," said Pandora. As he lit a cigarette, she put an envelope containing a dozen of the most interesting shots of the Minister for Regional Development on his desk.

"It will probably save time if you just look at these," she said, folding her hands primly in her lap.

Hudak looked at the envelope as if it were a pit viper.

"Go ahead," said Pandora, "it won't bite you. Unless I tell it to."

He reached over and picked the envelope up, turned it over in his hands thoughtfully, then took a dagger from his desk drawer and cut it open. He looked inside cautiously, then removed the prints and went through them. Pandora had edited the seventy shots down to a dozen, and he looked at each carefully, making little grunting noises and shaking his head at several. Finally, he sighed and threw them on his desk, pinching the bridge of his nose.

Pandora picked up the photos and shuffled through them to a photo of Hudak naked in the huge leather chair, gripping his cock in his fist. "This is my favorite," she smiled, a cat regarding a canary. "In America they call that jerking off. I don't know the Czech expression for it but I'm sure the political editor at Právo will. Your language is so colorful, I wouldn't be surprised if there's a specific term for it when the masturbator is the Minister for Regional Development."

He took a deep drag on his cigarette as she continued looking through the photos. "I love this one too," she said, showing him a photo of his ass framed by her thighs, his back striped with bloody scratches.

"Did you tell your wife you were berry picking, or maybe just attacked by a wild animal?"

Hudak took a last deep drag on the cigarette, stubbed it out, then sat forward in his chair, folding his hands in front of him.

"You're playing a dangerous game, Mrs. Krizova."

"So, I guess this is where I tell you that copies of these have already left the country, with instructions that they be sent to Právo if anything happens to me or my husband."

"I have no money," he said. "It's all my wife's."

"Oh, we don't want your money. But all this nonsense about the permits for Mr. Krizova's project will be immediately sorted out, with no more bullshit tennis matches."

"Tennis matches?"

"You really think you could beat him?"

The minister sat back in his chair. "And, of course, none of this matters if he's in prison so —"

Pandora finishes his sentence. "All the charges against my husband will be withdrawn, along with a formal apology, and our assets and property will be returned. I've written it all down, so there's no confusion."

She found a piece of paper in her bag and handed it to him. "In America we call this a laundry list. Goodness, you're learning some useful English terms today, aren't you?"

He leaned back in his chair to look it over.

"What makes you think I can do all this?"

"You'd better hope you can. Otherwise—" She picked up the photo of him gripping his penis and held it with both hands next to a photo of his wife. "You won't be just rich and powerful, you'll be famous."

Pandora stacked the photos neatly, smiling, then sat back and folded her hands in her lap.

"Well," she said, raising an eyebrow. "I don't have all day."

"Has your husband seen these?"

"No."

"It seems they would be as embarrassing for you as for me. Would you want him to see them?"

"Not especially," she said. "But I would risk much more to keep him out of a Czech prison and, while I haven't met the woman, I believe he might be a little more open-minded about these matters than your wife."

"The Pope is more open-minded than my wife," Hudak grumbled. "Very well, it will be taken care of."

"All," said Pandora.

"It will *all* be taken care of." he said, angrily.

"*Now*," said Pandora. "I want to see you pick up the phone and make the call. And if my husband isn't waiting for me when I get home I'm going straight to the fucking newspaper."

"All right!" he said, and she watched him squirming as he spoke to the prosecutor's office. When it was done, he looked at her. "Was that satisfactory?"

"If you read the list you'll see there's one more item. My assistant, Danka Medvedík was arrested for the crime of working in a lingerie shop. All record of her arrest will be expunged, and she will *not* be deported." Pandora stood and hung her bag from her shoulder. "*Now* we're done." She turned her back on him and went to the door.

"Mrs. Krizova."

Pandora stopped, her hand on the door knob.

"What assurance do I have there won't be more demands?"

"Because I'm not a shit, like you."

Demkakova nodded, impressed. "If your husband had the balls you have he would have had his permits months ago."

"I think you mean like yours, don't you, Minister?"

"I suppose I do," he said confidently.

"And I suppose, even after all of this, you'd like another fuck, wouldn't you? Maybe on your desk?"

Demkakova was suddenly alert, like a dog waiting for a thrown stick. "Could we?"

Pandora suddenly had a vision of his hairy white ass in the photo, and all the anxiety and tension of the previous week exploded in an uncontrollable fit of laughter.

"What? What is it?" demanded the minister.

"Nothing...everything," said Pandora, barely able to get the words out.

The minister's secretary, who had been listening at the door, hurried back to her seat as Pandora left the inner office, still cracking up.

Hudak's voice crackled over the intercom, "Miss Stanek, I need you in my office."

Confused, the girl looked at the insane laughing woman.

"You'd better hurry," Pandora said to her, blotting tears from her eyes, "or he'll have to take matters into his own hands."

§

Pandora wasn't sure it would, but her key worked in their front door. She took down the government notice, then closed the door behind her and sighed. The house had been roughly searched. She assumed anything of value would be gone. She decided to start with the kitchen, replacing the drawers and the silver and utensils. She wanted to have a nice dinner started when Ty arrived, but the cupboards were bare. All the wine was gone. They'd even taken the frozen steaks from the freezer; the only thing left in the fridge was Ty's pineapple juice, some wilted lettuce and a half-empty bottle of Champagne. She was afraid if she left to go shopping he'd come home to an empty house, so she got out two Champagne flutes, then removed the stopper from the bottle. The wine was completely flat. She slid to the floor with her back to the cabinet, exhausted.

She heard Ty come in the front door. She wanted to throw herself into his arms but couldn't summon the energy to stand. He saw her through the open kitchen door and she smiled. He put his jacket and briefcase down and walked into the kitchen. She offered him her hand for a lift. "Help me up, I don't have the strength left to do it on my own."

"Don't bother, I'll come down there," he said and slid down next to her. He put his arm around her and kissed her forehead, but she pulled his mouth to hers and held him there for the longest time.

He saw the Champagne glasses on the island and picked up the bottle beside her.

"Totally flat," she said. "And they cleaned out the wine rack."

"The house looks like it was hit by a tornado." "More like a pack of starving rats," said Pandora. "So, how was your day?"

Ty laughed at the incongruity of the question after the week they'd had. "Weird," he said, sliding the bottle away on the floor. I had a meeting scheduled with Vasek this afternoon but an hour before that a guard opened my cell door and told me they were cutting me loose. He, Vasek, was waiting outside. The prosecutor told him that Demkakova, the prick who framed me, changed his mind about testifying and all the charges have been dropped.

"Any idea why?" Pandora said, innocently.

"I don't have a clue."

And hopefully you never will, thought Pandora.

"But after this week, nothing could surprise me," Ty said, absently thinking about the seemingly impossible cock-up they appeared to have survived.

"I wouldn't be too sure about that," said Pandora, thinking about his permits.

"What?"

"I don't think they left us anything to eat, do you want to go out?"

"I do, I'm starving. Are you OK wearing what you have on?" he said.

"I haven't been upstairs to see if they left us any clothes and, frankly, I'm not prepared for that revelation. Let's go."

He helped her to her feet, and now she threw herself into his arms. "Have I told you lately that I love you?" she said, kissing him lavishly.

"No," he said, "but you had a good excuse, it has been a bit hectic."

"There's no good excuse for that," she said and kissed him again.

They went to Pandora's cafe, which was starting to feel like a second kitchen to her, and over wine and pasta he asked her what she wanted to do. "If you want to go back to California, we can."

"Is that what you want?" she said.

Ty thought about this before answering. "I thought so when I was in that cell. But now I can't help feeling that would mean the fucker won, even if he didn't." He searched her eyes for a clue to how she was feeling. "I mean, we've invested such a chunk of our lives in Prague. But none of that matters if you don't want to be here."

"I love it here," she said. "I love my shop, and our house and this funny city that feels like a huge fancy old music box. But most of all, I love you, and will go, or stay, wherever you want."

"I hoped you'd say that 'cause I'm not done here yet, I'm not even close to giving up."

She lifted her glass and toasted him. "My husband, my hero."

nine

The following week proved Pandora right. Ty was surprised when Vasek called with the news that the permits for his project had been approved. He'd looked at her pointedly. "It's almost like an angel has been watching over me."

She had no intention of letting him in on who his angel was, however his angel did make a call to Australia to tell Cerise they were fine and she wouldn't need to be mailing anything to a Prague newspaper. She asked her if she'd unsealed the envelope and

Cerise swore she hadn't, although they both knew her dear voyeur friend couldn't have resisted. Pandora just hoped she hadn't shown them to Malcolm.

The first order of business for the shop was to track down Danka but the police claimed to have no record of her arrest, and Pandora didn't have an address for her, either in Prague or Bratislava. She spent the better part of the rest of the day on the phone with her vendors in France, Germany, Switzerland and the UK calling in favors so she could quickly restock. By evening, she was wrecked, and she knew Ty would be too, finally moving onto the construction phase with his team, so she brought home chicken piccata and a bottle of claret from her cafe.

They ate by candlelight, both so tired she was afraid they'd fall asleep in their plates. But when she finally snuggled into him in bed and felt his hard cock pressed against her butt, she pushed him onto his back and lay her head on his belly, cupping his balls and sucking him like a baby holding a bottle. He stroked her hair gently as she worked his cock in her mouth, gratified to feel him tense as it throbbed his cum onto her tongue, and she swallowed, satisfied, falling asleep nearly as quickly as he.

§

Even with overnight delivery, it would be several days for the first shipments of fresh stock to arrive at the store. Pandora used this time to paint and replace the carpet and add some new fixtures. When it was done she went out to the street and looked in. Her pleasure at her handiwork was interrupted by a familiar voice. "Angelique."

Pandora turned around. It was Michal. *Shit.*

"*J'ai cherché pour toi partout Prague,*" he said, beaming.

"I'm sorry, I don't speak French," said Pandora in English.

"I don't understand," Michal said in heavily Czech-accented English. "Why you are talking to me this way? I know you are Angelique."

"I'm really not, Michal."

"You are Angelique, and I know because I am loving you."

"That's ridiculous, you don't know me."

"You are most wonderful woman I ever meet."

"We didn't meet. I'm not sure how to describe what we did but it wasn't meeting," said Pandora, her mind reeling.

"I don't care what you are, I am loving you."

"No you don't, because I'm not Angelique, I'm Mrs. Krizova, a married woman who loves her husband very much."

"How this can be?" he said, "how you are doing the things you did with us?"

"It was a dream, Michal," she said, "and now we're awake, and I love my husband and you love your countess."

"But I don't think I am loving her now," he said.

"I can't say I blame you for that, but it has nothing to do with me."

"But it is every to do with you," he said, anguished. "I am thinking about nothing but you since that night."

"That night was literally insane. Maybe in some good ways but insane none the less, and it was definitely not the foundation upon which one builds a lifetime partnership."

"I do not understand."

"I know," she said gently. "Look, if something as silly as that is enough to make you question whether you want to spend your life with Beatrice, maybe you're right, maybe you shouldn't marry her. But I was just the catalyst, the spark that started you wondering about this. Now do you understand?"

"Maybe," he said, grudgingly.

"Will you do me a favor, and if you really care about me please say yes. Will you let me be a dream again, and return to being a dream for me?"

He studied her face for a long moment, and finally nodded sadly. "OK," he shrugged, "if this must be."

"It must be. Thank you," said Pandora. She gave him a peck on the cheek and watched him walk away, hoping he wouldn't come popping up again.

§

When Jarda parked his brown UPS truck in front of the store and wheeled in the first set of boxes, Pandora nearly cried with relief. She was back in the game. But she really did cry when, while opening them and restocking the racks and shelves, Danka walked in the door.

After they'd hugged and Pandora fussed over her and assured her she still had a job, she asked her what had happened and where she'd been. Danka said she'd been at her apartment, afraid to leave for fear they would pick her up again and deport her, or worse. Pandora wanted to know what she meant by "or worse."

"What did they do to you, Danka?" Pandora asked, gently.

The girl couldn't look her in the face. "Why are police always such pigs?" she murmured, and Pandora hugged her again.

"I'm sorry Danka, you didn't deserve that," she said, then looked into her tear-streaked face. "But at least you won't be deported. Our attorney saw to that."

"Thank you," said Danka.

"You shouldn't be thanking me; you were an innocent bystander. Do you know what that means?"

"No," said Danka, and laughed, wiping her tears.

"It means you were just unlucky to get in the way of our troubles."

"OK," said Danka, finally managing a smile, "let's play store."

§

By the weekend, they'd cleaned things up and received enough merchandise that Pandora was confident they would have a grand reopening on Monday, so she suggested to Ty that they celebrate Saturday night with a special dinner at a very special and very expensive restaurant. Afterwards, they continued the celebration by making love voraciously, tearing into each other like honey badgers.

Sunday morning she woke alone with a wine head. Ty had gotten up early and quietly to play tennis. She'd never understand how he did it, but she was too restless to stay home. Someone had told her about an impromptu market in Ziskov, a mix of Gypsies, farmers, hippies and local craftsmen, and she put on a little t-shirt, jeans and running shoes for the walk, and set out on in the beautiful late-spring morning, stopping on the Charles Bridge to watch the boats. It was too early in the season for much interesting produce but she found some beautiful fresh porcini mushrooms. She was disappointed that there weren't more local craftsmen, most of the tables were piled with black-market electronics but she did find a lovely beaded bracelet among a pretty young Nigerian's wares spread out on a blanket, and some quick haggling cut the price in half.

She decided she'd seen everything there was to see at the market and bought a meat-filled pastry to eat on the bridge on her walk home. Then she saw Danka, looking through CDs on a table manned by a wizened Gypsy woman with a blond, curly-haired two-year-old playing at her feet. Danka was wearing a short loose floral smock with her black Mary Janes and huge red sunglasses, and she was holding a small bouquet of wildflowers wrapped in newspaper. Pandora thought, except for the sunglasses, she looked like a ridiculously tall three-year-old. The vendor put her pastry in a bag and she walked over to the table.

"Find anything interesting?" she said in English. Danka looked around, surprised and delighted to see her.

"Not really. I think they are...how do you say, not real?"

"Counterfeit."

"Yes, *patisk.*"

"Have you had lunch?"

"Just coffee. I was too late last night. I think maybe too much brandy," said Danka.

"This market is nice. I found something pretty."

"Let me see," said Danka, then clucked her tongue in approval when Pandora showed off her new bracelet. "I know this girl who sells these. She is sweet."

"You come here every Sunday?"

"I live near. This is my building," she said, pointing to an apartment building several blocks away. "Would you like to see? I can make us some tea."

§

Danka's apartment was a tiny studio with a nice sunny window. She took off her shoes when they entered, and Pandora immediately sat in a chair by the door and started to take off hers. "It's OK if you want to wear them," she said.

"No, I like to take them off inside too," said Pandora, looking around the room. The "closet" was a rod mounted in the corner beside a small bureau. A poster of Van Gogh's sunflowers was taped over a small bed. In the opposite corner sat a tiny desk beside brick and board shelves lined with books. A French grammar was open on the desk next to a dog-eared notebook and a French-Czech dictionary.

"You're learning French?" said Pandora, flipping through the grammar.

"A little. It's hard without a class."

"We can speak it at work if you like."

"I'd love that," said Danka, filling a vase for her flowers as Pandora went to the window, several stories above the traffic buzzing below.

"Do you like it, I mean, my apartment?" Danka asked.

"It's lovely. Where's your roommate?"

"She is gone."

"Where?"

"Moscow. She has been accepted in dance conservatory."

"That's wonderful for her but are you OK with it?"

"It's good. I was tired her immature."

Pandora hadn't thought too much about Danka's personal life. She knew she was a regular in the clubs weekends, and she was so pretty and with that body she assumed she probably had her choice of boys. For the first time, it occurred to her she might have Danka all wrong. For one thing, there was only one small bed in the apartment. She turned around and was surprised to find the girl closely in front of her, looking intently into her eyes. "Danka, is something wrong?" Pandora said gently.

"Nothing wrong," she said, and lifted her dress over her head, dropping it to the floor. Braless, as usual, Danka was naked now except for bikini panties. For a long moment Pandora could feel the girl's breath on her face, then Danka kissed her on the mouth.

Certainly Pandora wasn't shocked, after making love to Cerise three times (or was it four?), and she liked Danka very much and didn't want to embarrass her. She kissed her back as she stroked her hair in the friendliest possible manner, trying to think how to put it so as not to hurt her feelings. But Danka's amazing probing tongue made her lose her train of thought. It felt like an independently sentient being as it teased the tip of her tongue, caressing her mouth with a firmness and delicacy she'd never experienced. And it was so long.

Pandora's hands slid down her back to the curve of her ass, the muscles tight from thousands of hours of ballet, then up to her rib cage, stopping just short of her firm, lovely breasts, their nipples hard and pink as pencil erasers. Lightheaded, she pulled away.

"I...don't know what to say," began Pandora but Danka kissed her again.

"It is not complicate, I want pleasuring you," the girl murmured, nibbling at her lips.

"I know," said Pandora softly, "and that's wonderful but I'm married, you have to understand that."

"I know this," said Danka, softly kissing her lips and chin and cheeks and nose.

"I love my husband and I always will and I'll always be with him," said Pandora.

"I know this too," said Danka, taking her hand and leading her to the bed, where she lifted Pandora's t-shirt over her head. She sat on the bed and unhooked her bra, freeing her breasts, and fondling and kissing them as if it were something she'd been thinking about doing for a very long time. "You have so much," she said sucking on the nipples until they stood up like alert soldiers. She unbuttoned her jeans, Pandora swaying dizzily as Danka stripped her jeans from her hips. Kissing her belly, she twisted her onto the bed, where she finished pulling her jeans off. Danka started to remove Pandora's thong, but she was suddenly shy and they lay facing each other, Pandora once again feeling the girl's breath close on her face. She kissed her, now *her* tongue doing the exploring, thrilled at the feel of Danka's breasts and belly pressed against hers. Danka slid her leg between Pandora's, pressing her thigh against her pussy, and Pandora instinctively thrust against it.

Still they kissed, with happy sighs, then Danka's lips were on Pandora's cheeks and eyes, her neck and shoulders and her breasts, Danka burying her face between them, kissing and biting and licking them.

Since coming to work for Pandora, Danka had thought a lot about her employer's breasts. The first time Danka helped Pandora in the dressing room and Pandora had taken her bra off, Danka had ached to feel their firm fullness in her hands and take her nipples in her mouth. She would have died of embarrassment if Pandora had known she'd brought herself to climax thinking about the moment in the store's small lavatory afterward. Now she lavished them with months of stored up anticipation, as her seeking hand slid down her belly, then under the lace of her panties, her fingers across Pandora's clit and into her now wet vagina. Pandora gasped as they probed, then returned, nicely lubricated, to her clit, swelling under the girl's touch.

Danka kissed her belly, and Pandora looked down and their eyes met as she stroked the girl's hair. Danka smiled and kissed her hips and thighs, sliding her thong off. She pushed her legs apart, pressed her lips against her pussy, and spread her tingling labia to reveal her swollen clit and began to move it with her brilliant tongue. Pandora put her head back, her fingers in her own hair now, as Danka swirled her tongue around her clit. Then her fingers took over, still slick with sweet wetness, and her tongue slid down Pandora's labia to her glistening vagina, first flicking the lips, teasing, then pushing in, and Pandora shook as she felt the girl's tongue moving deeper in her than she ever imagined possible and in ways she'd never dreamt of.

Pandora writhed, the pleasure nearly unbearable, and Danka's tongue returned to her clit, licking it firmly as she inserted first one, then two, then three fingers in her vagina, moving them in rhythm with her tongue. Now Pandora thrashed, her moans becoming cries, and Danka pressed her mouth against Pandora's now rigid clit, shaking her head violently, until Pandora cried out, the muscles in her pussy clenching hard on Danka's fingers. Still Danka pressed on, and Pandora, now super-sensitive, stopped her, giggling. Danka looked up and smiled, and kissed her there again but gently, then turned around and lay beside her, kissing her on the mouth.

"My God, you're amazing" whispered Pandora, kissing her mouth, then her eyes and chin. She lifted her up until Danka was leaning over her and she cupped and squeezed her breasts, nuzzling and kissing them, licking and sucking the nipples until they were erect, pressing back against her tongue. She slid Danka's panties off her smooth dancer's ass, once again marveling at how tight and perfect the girl's body was. On her knees, Danka slipped her panties from her ankles, then straddled Pandora's chest. Cupping her breasts, she pressed her clit to each of Pandora's hard nipples, wetting them with her labia, then sliding her clit against them again. Seeing Danka's excitement, Pandora squeezed her breasts together so both nipples pressed against her swollen clit, and the girl fucked her bountiful tits, her fingers buried in her hair.

Holding the tight twin globes of the girl's ass, Pandora lifted her up until Danka straddled her face, and she pulled the girl's pussy to her mouth, exploring with her tongue as Danka moaned and moved slowly on her. Danka closed her eyes and hung her head back, riding Pandora's face as Pandora's tongue explored, first her clit, then gently down to her vagina and pushed inside, tasting her. Now Pandora spread her labia and flicked with her tongue, causing the girl to make kittenish cries. A moment of this was all

Danka could endure, and she held Pandora's head in her hands and pressed her clit hard against her mouth. Pandora responded in kind, sliding her hands up Danka's legs to her ass, encouraging Danka's thrusts.

Barely able to balance, Danka twisted around until her mouth found Pandora's pussy, kissing it as she continued to fuck Pandora's mouth. Newly aroused, Pandora moaned, thrilling to the return of Danka's tongue to her clit, and the women moved against each other in primal harmony, tongues and breathing in sync as they pushed each other higher until the warm flush of their orgasm found them.

For a quiet minute they lay thusly, like yin and yang (or, perhaps, yin and yin?), gently kissing each other in that most intimate manner, then Pandora pulled Danka up into her arms. They kissed soft kisses, Pandora struck by the mixture of their scents on their lips until finally she whispered. "I really like you."

"I am liking you very much too."

"But I also really like having you helping me in the shop. I mean, I wouldn't want anything to..."

Danka touched her lips. "Don't worry, I need this job too. But perhaps we might have tea again sometime?"

"Perhaps," smiled Pandora.

ten

It would never be said that Pandora's life was routine but between jam-packed days at the shop with Danka and lovely exhausted nights with Ty she started to enjoy a pleasant almost-domesticity. So, of course, she was relieved when she and Ty settled into the leather upper deck first class seats in the Air France 747 bound for Guadeloupe, the French West Indies, with a brief stop in Paris.

The plane lifted off and Pandora looked down on Prague, now most definitely her home, sparkling like a jewel in the summer morning. The seatbelt light blinked off and the flight attendant came to take their drinks. She was an adorable girl, and Pandora observed her clearly effected husband slyly, certain that the next time he fucked her she would get an extra hard pounding thanks to the memory of this delectable creature in her crisp Air France uniform.

"And for the Madame?" she said in French, snapping Pandora back to the moment.

"*Champagne, s'il vous plaît,*" said Pandora.

"I can't believe we're really doing it, taking a vacation," Ty said, utilizing his magic secret boy-vision to track the progress of the flight attendant's ass up the aisle.

"Thanks to Danka," said Pandora.

"Well, I was starting to worry, you've been working late with her almost every night. She was supposed to free up your time, not mean more work."

"She's just needed a little hands-on training?"

"I'm glad you're comfortable enough with her to leave her alone in the shop for two weeks."

"I've been amazed at how quickly she's picked it all up. And, I have to admit, I've learned a lot working with her too, I mean, about management."

"Well, anyway," he said, "it's just going to be you and me for two weeks, with nothing to do but eat, sleep, lie on the beach and—"

"Screw," Pandora whispered in his ear wickedly.

"I wouldn't have put it quite so poetically but yes, I'm planning on doing you silly," he said quite sincerely.

§

The pilot circled low enough before landing at Pointe-à-Pitre to give them a spectacular view of the emerald island's white sand beaches washed by crystal blue water. Ty rented a little white Japanese SUV and they drove south to Basse-Terre, the quiet side of the island, away from the frenzy of tourists and cruise ships, and as they passed ordinary townspeople in tiny cars, motorbikes, bicycles and even an old man on a donkey, Pandora remembered the delight she always felt at the miracle of travel in the jet age, how you can walk in the door of the aircraft, almost like entering an elevator and step out on another floor in an entirely different world.

Ty had promised her a "surprise within a surprise," the primary one being the trip to the "butterfly island." Unlike most of the former colonies in the Caribbean, Guadeloupe remained attached to its former European colonizer, and not just as a protectorate, Guadeloupe is a region of France, with deputies in the French National Assembly. Today, the Euro is their currency.

Using a map he'd bought at the airport, Ty navigated from the main road onto a narrow cobblestone path lined with towering palms to a sprawling, red-stained wood structure nestled in a glade of spreading tropical trees, ferns, and flowers.

"My God," said Pandora, "what is this place?"

"Le Hotel Jardin Enchanté," he smiled as he parked their jeep. "But this is just reception and the restaurant, you haven't seen anything yet."

The "anything" she hadn't seen yet was a thatched bungalow nestled at the point where the carpet of green that began at the top of La Grande Soufrière, the semi-active volcano on the left "wing" of the butterfly, rolled to the edge of a white sand beach washed by the most intensely blue tropical water Pandora had ever seen.

And Pandora acclimated very quickly. In barely the time it took to unpack and stow the mini sundresses, tiny shorts and tops and tinier bathing suits that comprised most of her luggage, she was floating in warm salty azure kissed by cerulean sky.

Suddenly ambitious, she rolled over and kicked into a polished breaststroke, not stopping until she reached the reef that guarded their cove, then floated onto her back again, kicking gently, feeling the sun on her face and tummy, until she sensed the sandy bottom nearing. She stood and looked at the two rattan chaises under an umbrella on the beach, where Ty was (for God's sake!) reviewing contracts from a stack in his briefcase sitting on a low table between the chaises.

Ty had just finished noting some recommended structural changes in red pencil when his dripping wet bikini-clad wife came running up the beach from the water and straddled him.

"Careful!" he said, unsuccessfully protecting the papers from her saltwater spray. "You're all wet!"

"You have no idea," said Pandora as she ripped the papers from his hands and dropped them in the briefcase. She pinned his shoulders and looked into his eyes.

"Probably time to knock off work, I guess," he shrugged, squinting up at the woman who was, at least, blocking the sun from his eyes.

"Unless you want me to kill you," said Pandora, seemingly quite serious.

"Well, we can't have that, can we? I mean, you spending the rest of your days rotting in a Caribbean dungeon."

"Do you like this bathing suit? I got it just for our trip," she said, displaying breasts barely contained by a kind of engineered macramé.

"Nice."

"Only nice? What about these?" she said, placing his hands on her breasts.

"Very nice."

"That's better," she said, leaning into his hands as she pressed her pussy against him until she felt the stirring in his baggy surfer shorts. She leaned forward and pressed her mouth on his, dry humping him like a high schooler, and his hand slid down to the bare cheeks of her ass, encouraging her thrusts.

Normally Ty hated coming in his pants but he let himself build to an orgasm, figuring he could just jump in the ocean. That is until he heard the beach waitress' golf buggy bringing icy cocktail glasses of Ti-Punch. Pandora slid off him, giggling, and he quickly covered his tented wet spot with a towel. The waitress, a leggy, high-cheekboned beauty with skin like polished ebony, covered her mouth to conceal her amusement as Ty dug some francs out of the pocket of his shorts for her, and said, "*Merci*," praying the money didn't smell like cum.

§

That night, after a day of paradisiacal solitude, they drove to Gourbeyre for seafood and nightlife, Pandora braless beneath a short white knit mini dress that was basically a long tank top. After fresh local lobsters in very French butter sauce washed down with a fat white Burgundy, they club-hopped, until they found the San Souci, a dance hall with high, red velvet padded booths surrounding a teaming dance floor and a Zouk DJ inspiring the frenzied dancers.

A waitress appeared, another thin, exotic beauty, wearing a brightly printed head scarf and a fringed cape tied over her hips. "Would you like something to drink?" she asked in thick Creole patois French, as she slapped napkins on the table in front of them.

"Champagne," said Ty, and she disappeared into the crowd with a matter of fact "*Très bonne.*"

"Dance with me!" said Pandora, grabbing Ty's hand and pulling him to the center of the pulsating throng. Moving to the music, she put her face close to his and lifted her hands over her head, raising her breasts and rolling her hips as her lips sought his. She spun against his chest until her ass was moving on his thighs, and they danced until they were glistening with sweat in the light humidity.

Ty put his hands on her hips, moving against her, then slid his hands lower. "Are you wearing panties?" he shouted in her ear.

"Commando," she smiled wickedly. "Shall we see if she's brought our Champagne?" she said, planning a surprise of her own.

She took his hand and they threaded their way back to the booth, but the table still only had the two napkins the waitress left. Pandora pushed him into the booth, lifted the skirt of her dress and straddled him, holding his head in her hands as she smothered him with kisses. She pressed her lips to his ear. "Do you want to know another fantasy I've always had?"

Ty got the idea, feeling the warm wetness of her pussy in his lap. He looked behind her. The booth was nearly enclosed and the crowd an anonymous wall of moving bodies. He unbuttoned his shorts and pushed them to his knees, then guided the tip of his already hard cock to the lips of her welcoming vagina. She kissed him hard as she felt it enter her, then lowered herself onto it, flattening her legs so it pressed deep inside her. Now they moved with the music, in pure harmony, completely alone in the crowd, their mouths locked, until their simultaneous cries pierced the din of Sans Souci.

Pandora collapsed against him, and they kissed gently as the DJ segued into another song. She slid off him to the cushioned seat of the booth, pulling her skirt down as he pulled up his shorts. Then they saw the linen napkin-wrapped bottle of Champagne in a perspiring silver bucket and two Champagne flutes on their table.

§

Of course they left the waitress an impressive gratuity for her discreet service. In fact, they were still laughing when they got back to the bungalow. They undressed for bed in the moonlight but Pandora, seduced by the sound of the waves lapping on the sand, pulled Ty to the water, where they delighted in the feel of the warm water on their naked bodies as they frolicked like dolphins. Then, neck deep, she wrapped her arms and legs around him, pressing her pussy against his hard cock, and they kissed for the longest time, the dappled reflection of the moonlight stretching from them to the horizon.

The eighty-degree temperature of the water was close to the air that night, and they stripped the blanket off the bungalow's bed and lay naked on the sheet. Pandora stretched across Ty's belly and stroked his cock thoughtfully, then took it in her mouth, scratching his balls as she performed her oral magic. Blissful, he traced the curve of her waist and hip with his hand, then slid around, pushing her onto her side and lifting her leg, kissing her clit and her quivering labia, pushing his tongue in her, then returning his lips to her clit, sucking and tonguing it gently as she sucked him in the moonlight until the perfectly attuned couple was warmed by the synchronicity of simultaneous orgasm and fell instantly asleep, Ty's cock still lightly suctioned in Pandora's mouth, and Pandora's clit still pressed against his lips.

Pandora woke in the tropically sudden first light of morning with Ty's cock in her mouth and feeling his head still resting on her inner thigh. She moved slightly and he stirred; his lips still pressed against her pussy. Knowing it was his favorite way to awaken, and since she couldn't think of a better way to start the day, she resumed her oral ministrations, and he stirred, realizing first where they were, then what they were about, and cheerfully joined the party.

§

Instead of room service breakfast, they ate in the hotel restaurant for a change, the fare typically French, excellent coffee, bread, and pastries, with fresh butter and jam served from a buffet. They took it out onto the veranda, with its view of the pool and the garden, overgrown with ferns and flowers.

"I've been thinking a lot, for the last few months, about our life together," said Ty as he buttered a croissant, exhibiting his maddening habit of discussing serious matters at random times as if it were part of an ongoing conversation.

"Really," said Pandora, having no idea where he was going with this.

"You know, I was a little worried about the crazy stuff we did in Prague, with Cerise and, you know, those two guys. But now I feel that sharing those experiences brought us closer. I mean, it isn't healthy to suppress fantasies. We need to think about and discuss them honestly, even sometimes give them some air, so they don't become obsessions."

"That is so true," said Pandora buttering a second croissant so airy and flaky it felt like a little cloud in her hand.

The concierge, Jean-Paul, appeared at their table. "*Excusez-moi, monsieur, vous avez un appel,*" he said apologetically. Ty dabbed his mouth with his napkin and went to take the call on the phone at the front desk.

Jean-Paul lingered, as he always did when it involved Pandora. Ty had laughingly told her he'd asked while they were checking in if she was a movie star. He smiled, brilliant white teeth framed by smooth ebony skin, as he topped up her cup from the coffee pot on their table.

"*Est-ce Madame besoin rien d'autre?*"

Guadeloupians were weirdly beautiful people, she thought, almost like a nation of fashion models. Like many of the young men on the island, Jean-Paul had a weightlifter's build but in the week they'd been there she hadn't seen any locals doing anything resembling exercise. On their third day, Jean-Paul brought a breakfast tray while Ty was in the shower. Pandora was already in a bikini but he'd been shy, too polite to look at her in the honestly sexual way the islanders did each other. What if he'd known that at that moment she'd wanted to kneel in front of him and press her hand on the big cock whose subtle outline she'd discerned beneath his loose cotton trousers, then when his pants could barely contain his erection, pull them from his waist and, bracing herself on his muscled quads, stretch her lips around the tip and suck until he filled her mouth with a gush of creamy, sweet cum?

"*Non, merci,*" she replied, smiling as she thought, *Ty was right, it's so important not to suppress our fantasies.*

She picked up the cup and took a sip as a hummingbird deftly probed the purple labia of the flowers on the passion fruit vine encircling the pillars of the veranda.

Ty returned, looking worried, sat down and spread the napkin in his lap. "It was Tom," he said, referring to his twin. "Jennie's left him."

"Oh dear," said Pandora, as she picked up the coffee pot and refilled his cup, carefully holding the lid. "Poor Tom. Is he OK?"

"I'm afraid not. It's hit him pretty hard, I've never heard him so blue. Honey, I know this was supposed to be our alone time but I invited him to join us."

"No worries," said Pandora, placing the pot back on the tray, "we'll have fun doing things together."

Considering the possibilities, she settled back and bit into her perfect croissant, as the hummingbird probed an exceptionally succulent blossom.

www.ingramcontent.com/pod-product-compliance
Lightning Source LLC
Chambersburg PA
CBHW050930120626
46552CB00001B/132